The Bluebeard Room

A creaking noise echoed from the corridor. What on earth is that? Nancy wondered. Her bedside clock showed 1:17 A.M. She threw back the covers and pulled on a robe and slippers. Then she peered out of her room down the hall.

It was Lisa! Nancy called out to her softly but got no response.

Her friend went up the tower stairs, and Nancy realized that Lisa was walking in her sleep! Her own skin chilled to gooseflesh at the eerie sight.

A gasp of horror rose in Nancy's throat as she suddenly sensed her friend's intention. Already Lisa was climbing up into the opening in the parapet.

Another moment and the sleepwalker would be poised to step off into empty air!

Nancy Drew
Mystery Stories

#57 The Triple Hoax
#58 The Flying Saucer Mystery
#59 The Secret in the Old Lace
#60 The Greek Symbol Mystery
#61 The Swami's Ring
#62 The Kachina Doll Mystery
#63 The Twin Dilemma
#64 Captive Witness
#65 Mystery of the Winged Lion
#66 Race Against Time
#67 The Sinister Omen
#68 The Elusive Heiress
#69 Clue in the Ancient Disguise
#70 The Broken Anchor
#71 The Silver Cobweb
#72 The Haunted Carousel
#73 Enemy Match
#74 The Mysterious Image
#75 The Emerald-eyed Cat Mystery
#76 The Eskimo's Secret
#77 The Bluebeard Room
#78 The Phantom of Venice
#79 The Double Horror of Fenley Place
#80 The Case of the Disappearing Diamonds
#81 The Mardi Gras Mystery
#82 The Clue in the Camera
#83 The Case of the Vanishing Veil

Available from MINSTREL Books

NANCY DREW®

THE BLUEBEARD ROOM

CAROLYN KEENE

A MINSTREL® BOOK

PUBLISHED BY POCKET BOOKS

New York   London   Toronto   Sydney   Tokyo

A Minstrel Book published by
POCKET BOOKS, a division of Simon & Schuster Inc.
1230 Avenue of the Americas, New York, N.Y. 10020

Copyright © 1985 by Simon & Schuster Inc.
Cover artwork copyright © 1988 by Bob Berran
Produced by Mega-Books of New York, Inc.

ISBN: 0-671-66857-9

First Minstrel Books printing August, 1988

10 9 8 7 6 5 4 3 2 1

Contents

1	A Strange Chat	1
2	The Stone Arrowhead	8
3	Witch Lore	14
4	Rock Idol	22
5	Press Party	31
6	Powder Bag	39
7	Surprise Meeting	48
8	An Unexpected Visitor	57
9	A Night on the Town	65
10	A Haunted Land	73
11	Spook Attack	81
12	Danger in the Dark	92
13	A Whispered Warning	101
14	Night Sight	113
15	Undine	119
16	The Grotto Symbol	128
17	Secret Altar	136
18	Witch Bane	146

1

A Strange Chat

"Guess who's at the party, Nancy!"

"About half the population of Long Island, I should think." Grinning, Nancy Drew gazed around at the guests. Some were dancing under a striped pavilion, while others chatted or sauntered about the lawn. Their talk and laughter, mingled with the strains of music, made it difficult to be heard.

"No, be serious, Nan—guess who!"

"I *am* serious, Bess. I've met about a dozen people just in the last few minutes, and I doubt that I'll remember any of their names when we leave."

"You'll remember *this* person's name," Bess Marvin declared firmly.

"All right, I give up." The strawberry blond's sapphire eyes twinkled. "Who's here?"

"Lance Warrick!"

1

"The rock star?" Nancy's eyes opened wide.

"How many Lance Warricks are there?" Bess was thrilled.

"Wow! If you're right, we may be in for a mob scene!"

The teenage detective was something of a celebrity herself, yet even she couldn't help feeling a tingle of excitement at the chance of meeting the popular British rock star in person. Lance Warrick had that effect on most girls. His group, the Crowned Heads, was just winding up a sensational concert tour of the United States.

"Have you actually seen him, Bess?"

"Not yet, but somebody said he just went by the pavilion, so George is trying to spot him."

Georgia Fayne, nicknamed George, was Bess's cousin.

"Aren't you glad we came, now?" Nancy teased. "Remember how George kept saying this party would be a terrible bore?"

"I know! Oh, Nancy, if we'd missed such a chance, I never would've forgiven myself!"

Nancy giggled at her plump blond friend's quivering enthusiasm. While visiting Nancy's Aunt Eloise in New York City, the three girls had been invited to a charity garden party given by a women's university club to which her aunt belonged. The party was being held in a white-columned mansion overlooking the blue waters of Long Island Sound, and so far the girls had enjoyed every minute of it.

Lance Warrick would be a terrific added attraction. "Is his whole group here, or just the king himself?" Nancy inquired.

"I don't know—but wouldn't it be thrilling if we could meet *all* the Crowned Heads?" Bess gushed. "Wait! Here comes George now!"

Georgia Fayne could hardly have been more different from her cousin. A pretty, trim-figured girl with short dark hair, she was as active and adventurous as her boyish nickname suggested.

"Well, did you see Lance Warrick?" Nancy asked with a grin.

"He's back at the pavilion again, dancing with one of the clubwomen," said George, "but you should see all those idiot debs waiting to cut in!"

Bess dimpled. "You wouldn't stoop to such tactics yourself, I presume?"

"Only if I could find some way to cut them all out. By the way, Nancy, here's something for you." George handed her a folded note.

"What's this?"

"Don't ask me. Remember that servant in the white jacket who recognized you when we arrived?"

"The one who held the car door open for us?"

George nodded. "He said a friend was looking for you, and asked me to give you this."

Since the girls were strangers on the Island, and her Aunt Eloise had another engagement which had prevented her from attending the party, Nancy couldn't imagine who the friend might be.

3

The note was on monogrammed cream vellum, evidently torn from a purse pad:

Nancy, can we talk for a few moments? I'll be waiting by the refreshment table nearest the garden.

Olive Harwood

Nancy gave a little exclamation of surprise. "It's from Mrs. Harwood! Remember her?"

"Of course," said Bess. "She used to be a neighbor of ours back in River Heights."

"Moved to New York, didn't she," George added, "after her daughter married that Englishman?"

"That's right. She wants to talk to me about something. Keep an eye on developments with Lance Warrick, you two—I'll be right back!"

Nancy started off across the lawn, weaving her way among the party guests. Presently she caught sight of her former neighbor. The straw-hatted society matron looked rather grave and thoughtful but broke into a smile of greeting as the teenager approached. "Nancy, dear!"

"Why, Mrs. Harwood! How nice to see you again! How does Lisa like married life in England?"

"I wish I could say she was ecstatically happy, Nancy, but the truth is I'm worried about her. That's why I wanted to talk to you."

Shortly before the widowed Mrs. Harwood had

4

moved to New York, her only child, Lisa, had married an English aristocrat named Hugh Penvellyn. Their wedding had been one of River Heights' most festive and fashionable in recent years.

It was obvious to everyone that the couple were deeply in love. And the fact that, after their honeymoon, they would be settling in the groom's ancestral castle gave the whole affair an aura of fairytale romance. But now it sounded as though the two might not be living happily ever after.

"Is anything wrong?" Nancy's keen eyes searched the other's face sympathetically.

"I'm very much afraid so." Mrs. Harwood sighed. "Yet, I seem to be groping in the dark—that's what's so frustrating, Nancy. I can't imagine what could possibly have come between Lisa and Hugh."

"Have you seen them since the wedding?"

"Yes, I flew to London at Christmas time. That's when I first realized something was troubling Lisa."

"She's still in love with Hugh, surely?"

"Oh, more than ever! In fact, when I suggested she come back to New York with me for a week or so, Lisa wouldn't hear of it. It seemed she couldn't bear to be parted from him, even for that long."

Nancy was puzzled. "Then what makes you think anything's amiss?"

"The way she looks and acts—everything about her. You know how gay and lively Lisa always was. Well, now she seems totally changed. Her eyes are

5

absolutely haunted, Nancy. She acts as though some terrible secret is weighing on her mind, dragging down her spirits. She looks dreadful!"

Nancy suggested they sit on a garden bench and brought two glasses of punch from the refreshment table. Meanwhile, Mrs. Harwood opened her handbag and took out an airmail envelope with a British stamp. In it was a colored snapshot, which she handed to Nancy as Nancy handed her one of the glasses of punch.

The teenager studied the photo with interest. It showed Lisa in the foreground, her blond hair streaming in the breeze. Penvellyn Castle loomed behind her on a grassy headland, with the vivid blue sea sparkling below in the summer sunshine.

"What a beautiful place to live!" Nancy said. "The castle's in Cornwall, isn't it?"

"Yes, in the southwest of England. But it's Lisa herself I wanted you to see. Can't you tell just by looking at her that she's unhappy?"

The attractive blond girl whom Nancy had known all through their school years had certainly changed —and judging by the photo, not for the better. She seemed thinner, almost haggard, and her slanting green eyes had dark circles.

"Lisa doesn't look herself, that's for sure," Nancy agreed. "Perhaps she's homesick."

"Then why won't she come back, if only for a short visit?" Mrs. Harwood shook her head, her eyes clouded with concern. "No, I'm convinced it's far more serious than that."

"Do you and Lisa keep in close touch?"

"Oh, yes! We correspond frequently and talk on the phone every few days . . ." Olive Harwood seemed to want to say something else. At last she blurted, "Nancy, will you treat what I'm about to say in absolute confidence?"

"Of course, Mrs. Harwood. You wouldn't be confiding in me if you didn't know that already. What is it?"

"Am I being foolish to wonder if . . . if . . . well, if Hugh may secretly be *poisoning* my daughter?"

2

The Stone Arrowhead

For a moment Nancy was too shocked to reply. The sedate society matron looked deadly serious.

"What on earth makes you think he might want to kill Lisa?" Nancy asked incredulously.

"It's not as fantastic as it may sound," Mrs. Harwood persisted. "Many of these titled Englishmen, from what I hear, haven't enough money to keep up their huge estates. And Lisa's a rich girl in her own right. Her grandfather left a fortune to her, which came under Lisa's full control when she turned twenty-one. So now, if anything happened to her, that money would all go to her husband."

"Has Lisa seen a doctor recently?"

"She says she has, and tells me he found nothing wrong. But I'm terribly afraid she may be covering up . . . for Hugh's sake."

8

Nancy scarcely knew how to respond. "You met him during their engagement, Mrs. Harwood. Were you suspicious of Hugh then? Surely he didn't strike you as a potential murderer?"

"No, I must admit he didn't . . . but that was before I saw this dreadful change in Lisa."

Nancy shook her head doubtfully. "I'm afraid I find the idea awfully hard to accept."

"But what other explanation is there?"

"I don't know, but there may be some perfectly simple reason."

"Find it, then!"

Nancy's blue eyes widened in surprise. "What exactly are you saying, Mrs. Harwood?"

The older woman laid a hand on Nancy's arm. "My dear, the two of you have been friends for years, and Lisa thinks the world of you. She always spoke as if there were no situation you couldn't handle, no mystery that Nancy Drew couldn't solve. Won't you please look into this one, if only to put my mind at ease?"

Nancy was touched. "I'm happy Lisa feels that way, Mrs. Harwood, and flattered that you should ask me to help. But really—Lisa's in England, and I'll soon be going home to River Heights. How can I possibly find out what's wrong?"

"That's no problem, my dear. You could fly to England for a week or two at my expense. When Lisa hears you're coming, she's sure to invite you to visit her in Cornwall. That way, you can see for yourself how she and Hugh are getting along, and decide if there are any grounds for my suspicions."

Nancy had no immediate plans for the summer, and the idea of a trip to England was certainly tempting. She loved London, and right now it was an exciting source of trendy new fashions, new music and new life styles.

All the same, she felt deep misgivings about prying into Lisa's marriage. Her knack for solving mysteries had made the name of Nancy Drew well known to the public, and had brought the teenage sleuth intriguing cases from points far beyond River Heights. But none of her cases had ever involved her in problems between a husband and wife.

"Do say you will, my dear!" pleaded the older woman as she picked up the envelope to replace her daughter's photograph in it.

"I don't know what to tell you, Mrs. Harwood, but to be honest, I feel—"

Nancy broke off as she saw something fall onto her friend's lap. "Where on earth did that come from?" she inquired softly.

It looked like a tiny arrowhead, about an inch long, carved from some sort of glassy stone. Olive Harwood picked it up between her thumb and forefinger.

"It was in the envelope when I first opened it," she replied. "I wondered myself, but there wasn't a word about it in Lisa's letter, so I suppose it must've gotten into the envelope by accident. . . . Odd little thingamajig!"

She went on as Nancy studied the object with a troubled frown. "Looks rather Stone-age, doesn't it?—like one of those ancient artifacts archeologists dig up."

Nancy nodded absently, absorbed in her thoughts. She had once read about an English farmer plowing up a gold ornament dating back to the days of King Alfred.

With a sigh, her former neighbor returned to the subject that was uppermost in her mind. "Anyhow, my dear, please say you will visit Lisa!"

"Let me think about it, and I'll give you a definite answer tomorrow. . . . And may I keep this . . . thingamajig for the time being?"

Mrs. Harwood smiled and patted her hand. "Of course, Nancy! And now let me ask something else—would you like to meet Lance Warrick?"

The pretty teenager flashed a smile. "What girl wouldn't? Can you arrange it?"

"I can do better than that. I'll introduce you personally!" Taking Nancy by the hand, she rose and drew her back toward the party.

"You're serious?" Nancy asked as they left their glasses at the table and started across the lawn.

"Absolutely! I'm one of the people who persuaded him to come here today. I thought it might help ticket sales—he's promised to preside over the raffle, you see."

11

"You know Lance Warrick?" Nancy asked in surprise.

"My son-in-law does. I suppose you could call that one of the fringe benefits that go with a titled English connection."

Many of the guests were now clustering around the pavilion. Evidently word had spread that the British rock star was among the dancing couples. Although two other members of his group were also on hand, he was the focus of all eyes.

The music of the garden party orchestra was tame and conventional compared to the rock group's. Yet Lance seemed to fit in and dominate the scene naturally. In his white silk suit, with his lavender shirt and tie and spiky blond hair, he was instantly recognizable—an impish mixture of Mick Jagger, Billy Idol and David Bowie.

At the same time, Lance Warrick was, as always, uniquely himself—and outrageously handsome!

Nancy was suddenly annoyed at herself for thinking so. Her attitude toward the rock star had abruptly changed. He was acting too much like the lord of the manor, she felt—dancing with one girl after another, while all the rest stood oohing and aahing around the fringes, eagerly hoping to catch Lance's eye.

George was right, thought Nancy—they *are* idiots! Do I really want to be one of them?

Lance had just noticed Mrs. Harwood and was blowing her a kiss. She waved her fingers gently

12

and put an arm around Nancy, to draw his attention to the titian-haired teen.

Lance winked at her and smiled back at the older woman. "Be right with you, Olive darling!"

Nancy blushed as a dozen girls looked daggers at her. She could imagine their envious thoughts, wondering why she should be favored with the rock king's attention ahead of them.

Lance swung his current partner carelessly away into the waiting arms of his drummer, Bobo Evans. Then he started jauntily toward Mrs. Harwood and her attractive young companion.

Nancy abruptly turned away from the pavilion.

Mrs. Harwood called out, "Nancy dear, where are you going? Lance wants to dance with you!"

"No, thanks. Tell him I appreciate the honor, but I'd rather have another glass of punch."

3

Witch Lore

Eloise Drew lived in a charming old Victorian apartment building on the Upper West Side of Manhattan. With its turrets and gargoyles and crenelated ramparts, it looked like something out of a Gothic horror movie, but Nancy loved its spacious, high-ceilinged rooms and romantic atmosphere.

"Well, I hear you put the King of Rock in his place yesterday," her aunt joked as Nancy emerged from the guest room next morning.

Bess and George had already beaten her to the breakfast table.

"Something tells me a couple of gossipy little tongues have been wagging," said Nancy, grinning at her two chums.

"No, actually it was Olive Harwood who told me."

14

"Oh, my! I hope I didn't embarrass her." Nancy looked contrite as she took a chair.

"Not to worry, my dear. She thought you showed a splendidly independent spirit."

"She did! You should have seen her, Miss Drew," put in George Fayne. "Here were all these swooning females ready to fling themselves at Lance Warrick's feet, and Nancy gives him the brush-off!"

"But what a waste!" Bess lamented. "The chance of a lifetime and she passes it up!"

"And was he ever surprised!" George chuckled. "The poor guy was stunned. He couldn't *believe* that any girl would actually decline the thrill of dancing in his glamorous embrace!"

Nancy winced. "I *was* a bit rude."

"Baloney! It did him good. He was really getting too arrogant for words, the way he was carrying on there in the dance pavilion!"

"He'd have to be pretty unusual *not* to have his head turned by all that attention." Nancy helped herself to a slice of toast. "I must say he seemed nice enough when we talked later on."

In fact, Nancy felt ashamed of her display of temper. Lance had come upon her later in the evening in their host's mansion and had insisted on escorting her through the food line. Not only had he proven himself a charming conversationalist—he'd refrained from even mentioning the abrupt way Nancy had turned her back on him in the pavilion.

15

Aunt Eloise smiled and poured herself more coffee. "Well, at any rate, he sounds like a very interesting young man. By the way, Nancy, Olive Harwood asked me to remind you to call her about what you discussed yesterday."

"Oh, yes! I'm glad you did, Aunt Eloise." Nancy suddenly turned serious. "Which reminds me of something else. What's the name of that bookstore in Greenwich Village . . . ?"

"Which bookstore, dear?"

"The occult one, where you got me that book about the lore of the mandrake root. Afterward, when I was trying to find more information, the proprietor went to all sorts of trouble to help me."

"Nigel Murgatroyd, you mean, and his shop's called Merlin's Den. He's an elderly Englishman— worked as an archeologist, I understand. A really interesting fellow! But why do you ask, dear?"

"I'd like to go see him today and . . . look around his shop," Nancy ended vaguely.

"Don't tell us you're onto another mystery case?"

The teen sleuth smiled and shrugged off George's question. "Not exactly . . . or not yet, anyhow."

"But I thought we were going shopping," Bess protested.

"You two go ahead and I'll join you for lunch at Bloomie's at noon. We'll still have the whole afternoon."

The three girls caught a southbound Broadway-

Seventh Avenue subway train. Bess and George got off at 50th Street, within walking distance of Rockefeller Center and the glamorous Fifth Avenue window-shopping milieu. Nancy rode on downtown to the Village.

Merlin's Den was a dark hole-in-the-wall shop with little hint outside of the mysterious treasures within.

Unlike some of Manhattan's trendier occult bookstores, this one offered no tarot cards, Ouija boards or herbal displays. But its shelves were stocked with a vast array of arcane volumes, many of them rare and long out of print.

An immensely fat man with a gray mustache and goatee came forward. "May I help you, Miss?" His lively amber eyes narrowed in a frown of puzzled interest. "I say, have we met before?"

Nancy's own sapphire-blue eyes twinkled back at him. "No, but we've spoken on the phone. I'm Nancy Drew."

"Ah! Hello Miss Drew! How wonderful finally to meet you."

As he squeezed her hand warmly, she went on, "I happen to be in New York and need some more information, so I thought I'd stop in and avail myself again of your vast knowledge of the occult."

Nancy's formal little speech seemed to strike just the right note.

"How charming, how delightful!" the fat bookman beamed. "I can't imagine anything that would delight me more on this lovely summer's day!"

He insisted on drawing her back into the dim, cool recesses of his crowded store, toward a corner containing his littered rolltop desk, office chair and an ancient, chintz-covered rocker.

He sat Nancy down on the rocker, made some tea, then said, "Now, tell me your problem!"

The titian-haired teenager opened her shoulder bag and fished out the tiny arrowhead that had fallen from Mrs. Harwood's airmail letter.

The effect on Nigel Murgatroyd was striking. His eyes widened and he caught his breath sharply. He picked up the small object from Nancy's open palm, grasping it gingerly between his thumb and forefinger, as if it were some live, poisonous specimen.

"Do you know what this is?" he asked.

"I think so. It was sent to a friend of mine."

"From England? . . . But yes, of course—it must have been. . . . Well, my dear, as you've doubtless guessed, this is what's called an *elf-dart* or *elf-bolt*. A peculiarly British witch-weapon."

"Meant to do harm? . . . Psychological harm?"

"Oh, definitely! But not *just* psychological. These deadly little toys have been known to kill."

"Are you serious?"

Murgatroyd shrugged. "If one believes in them, at any rate. Even if one doesn't, they often lead to dire results, it would seem. For instance, Mary, Queen of Scots' foreign lover, Rizzio, and her

18

second husband, Lord Darnley, were both targets of elf-darts shortly before they were murdered."

Nancy shivered in spite of her common sense.

The bookshop owner went on, "Any way you look at it, my dear, this little stone arrowhead is a nasty bit of work. You may take it from me—someone wishes your friend evil."

Nancy was silent a moment as she returned it to her handbag. "And who might have sent my friend such a thing? . . . A modern witch?"

He nodded, frowning. "That's the likeliest answer. In olden times, it was the faerie folk—the little people—who supposedly zinged them at anyone they didn't like. The victim was said to be *elfshot*. But later on it was usually witches who were accused of using elf-bolts. You'll find them mentioned again and again in accounts of the witch trials."

"What can you tell me about witches, Mr. Murgatroyd?"

"Well, even today, historians and anthropologists aren't quite sure what to make of witchcraft. Some say it's what's left of the old religion that the early peoples of Europe believed in before they were converted to Christianity. *Wicca* is what the witches themselves call their craft. They believe they're making use of the forces of nature to help or harm people. The good ones practice 'white magic.' Elf-darts, needless to say, are examples of 'black magic.'"

19

"You believe witchcraft still exists?" Nancy asked.

"No doubt about that, my dear. I've personally witnessed witchcraft rites. And in the British Isles, I can assure you there are witch covens that have existed secretly for hundreds of years, even during times when belonging to one might result in being burned at the stake."

The fat man rose and fetched a book from one of the shelves. "Here, read this. It should answer any questions you may have on the subject."

Nancy glanced at the book's spine curiously and turned to the title page. *Wicca: The Way of Wisdom.* It had been printed at Oxford in 1907.

"How much do I owe you for this?"

Nigel Murgatroyd looked hurt. He raised a pudgy hand. "My dear Miss Drew, how can you ask? It's my very great pleasure to assist America's most attractive young mystery-solver!"

Bess and George were both flushed with excitement when Nancy joined them for lunch at Bloomingdale's.

"Ohmigosh, Nan! You should see the goodies they have on display here!" Bess exclaimed.

"Out of this world!" George confirmed. "I can easily imagine shoppers having a mental breakdown trying to decide what to buy!"

"In that case," Nancy laughed, "save your money and avoid the risk."

By the time the trio returned to Aunt Eloise's apartment, all three were laden with parcels.

Nancy giggled as her aunt cocked an amused eyebrow at their purchases. "Bawl *them* out for extravagance, Aunt Ellie—I have an excuse."

"Indeed? You must tell me about it—but later, please, after I've fortified myself with a sip of the homemade blackberry cordial Hannah sent me."

Hannah Gruen was the Drews' housekeeper, who had cared for Nancy devotedly ever since the untimely death of Mrs. Drew when Nancy was only three.

"In the meantime," Eloise Drew said as she picked up a plain brown envelope, "here's something that came for you this afternoon."

"Oh, thank you," said Nancy. "What's in it?"

"Haven't the vaguest idea. It came by messenger."

Nancy was puzzled as she saw the writing on the envelope. One address had been crossed out and another substituted. "How odd. This was first sent to that house on Long Island where the party was held, and then re-directed here, Aunt Eloise."

"Yes, so I noticed."

There was, however, no return address. Nancy opened the envelope and plucked out the contents.

"Well, come on! Don't keep us in suspense!" begged Bess, intrigued by the astonished look on her friend's face. "What is it?"

"Three tickets to the Crowned Heads farewell concert at Madison Square Garden!"

21

4

Rock Idol

"The Crowned Heads concert!" Bess's plump cheeks were suddenly pink with fresh excitement.

Nancy nodded, trying not to betray the fact that her own pulse had quickened. "Don't ask me how good the seats are, though. I'm not too sure what these letters and numbers stand for."

"May I see?" asked George, who knew the Garden seating plan from a previous rock concert. "Hey! These are *front row center!*"

She stared breathlessly at her titian-haired chum. "Nancy dear, do I get a teeny-weeny impression that *three* seats mean Bess and I are included in the invitation?"

"Certainly looks that way. Unless Aunt El—"

Miss Drew thrust out her hands in protest.

"Don't look at me, you all! My darling niece knows very well I'm no rock fan!"

"Wow!" cried Bess. "Do you realize Crowned Heads tickets for seats nowhere near as good are being scalped for a hundred bucks apiece?! I heard it on the TV news!"

"May I ask where these tickets come from," Aunt Eloise inquired, "if I'm not being too naive?"

"Three guesses!" laughed Bess, causing Nancy to dimple and blush slightly.

Her aunt smiled. "Well! You must have made quite an impression on young Mr. Warrick."

"I wouldn't know about that, but I do know one thing," said Nancy, eager to change the subject.

"Oh yeah? Like what?" asked George.

"The concert's tonight, which means we have about half an hour to eat dinner, shower and get dressed!"

Frantic activity followed, with the three girls squirming past each other as they ran back and forth between guest room and bathroom.

"How on earth do you youngsters do it?" Miss Drew wondered aloud. "If I'd just come back from a day's shopping, I'd be ready for an early bedtime or several hours snoozing in an armchair!"

"I think Bess must be snoozing in the tub," complained George. She rapped sharply on the bathroom door. "For heaven's sake, Bess, please hurry up. You've been soaking for ages!"

"Look who's talking!" Bess's voice echoed off the

tiled walls. "At least I don't spend hours admiring myself in the bathroom mirror!"

"Naturally," George retorted, "since you have so little to admire!"

Nancy giggled, knowing their insults were all in fun.

Later, Nancy had just finished putting on her earrings and touching up her lip gloss when she remembered about Mrs. Harwood. "Oh dear, I must call Mrs. Harwood before we go!"

Bess glanced fretfully at her watch. "Must you, Nancy? We haven't much time if we want to be on time for the concert!"

"It'll be too late to phone by the time we get back. Don't worry, I'll make it brief. Only I must call Daddy, too."

"Why?" asked George.

"To let him know I may be going to England."

There were gasps of surprise.

"And that's another reason why you two should try to get along," Nancy added with a teasing grin. "You may have only each other's company on the plane home tomorrow!"

Turning to her aunt, the teenager asked, "Okay if I use the phone, Aunt Eloise?"

"Of course, my dear. So this was your excuse for all the clothes-shopping this afternoon?"

"You've guessed it," Nancy twinkled.

The Drews' housekeeper answered Nancy's call

to River Heights. "Oh, Nancy, how good to hear from you! Are you having fun in New York?"

"Loads, Hannah! And I found one of those woks in the size you wanted, in Chinatown. It's being shipped out right from the store."

After a further fond exchange between the two, Nancy's father, the distinguished attorney Carson Drew, came on the line.

"How was the law seminar, Dad?" Nancy asked.

"Stuffy, but I dare say we all learned a few things. What's going on in Manhattan?"

"A rock concert tonight, as a matter of fact, so I must make this quick. You may not be seeing me at dinner tomorrow, Daddy." Nancy told him about Mrs. Harwood's unusual request. "I wasn't keen on going at first, but now I think I will."

"By all means do, honey. It should be a real summer treat. I know how much you like London, and Cornwall's the loveliest corner of England."

"What bothers me is not telling Lisa my real reason for coming. I hate the thought of snooping on her and her husband."

"If she herself invites you to Cornwall for a visit, I think your conscience can be clear."

"I hope so. Daddy, you've known Mrs. Harwood for years. What's your opinion of her?"

"Very level-headed, or so she always seemed to me. Takes after her father, old Sam Austin. He was a banker here in River Heights, you know. As a

25

matter of fact, I helped draw up the terms of the trust fund when he left most of his fortune to Lisa."

"Really? Mrs. Harwood says if anything happened to Lisa, all her money would go to Hugh Penvellyn. Is that right?"

"Yes, I assume so, now that she's twenty-one, unless—Hmm . . ." Mr. Drew's voice trailed off.

"Are you there, Dad?"

"Yes, I was just racking my memory . . . Seems to me there might be some special clause in the terms of the trust that could prevent it, but I'm hanged if I can remember what it was, at the moment."

"Never mind, you can let me know later, Daddy. Thanks for the information. We're in kind of a hurry, so I'd better sign off now. Lots of love!"

Next, Nancy called Olive Harwood and told her she was prepared to go to England.

"Oh Nancy, I'm so glad to hear that! How soon?"

"Whenever you like. Tomorrow even, if it's possible to get a flight on such short notice."

"I'm sure it is. My travel agent's marvelous," Mrs. Harwood replied. "She seems to have a sixth sense for ferreting out cancellations."

"Great! I'll be standing by."

"I'll have her book you a room at Claridge's in London, so Lisa will know where to reach you. Incidentally, I called her yesterday, right after we talked. I wanted to let her know as soon as possible that you might be coming."

26

"How did she react?"

"She was delighted! She's just dying to see someone from back home, especially an old friend like you. She thinks so much of you, Nancy!"

"Well, I feel the same way about Lisa, so I'll look forward to seeing her again, Mrs. Harwood."

Nancy hung up, excited by the thought of her upcoming trip abroad and hoping she'd made the right decision. George and Bess were waiting to whisk her out the door.

The girls had no trouble flagging a cab and were soon whizzing down Broadway. At Times Square in the glittering heart of the theater district, the taxi turned onto Seventh Avenue. Traffic was already very heavy. By the time their driver turned right toward the round, glowing modernistic bulk of Madison Square Garden, everything had slowed to a crawl.

"Good grief! Is it always like this on a concert night?" Bess gulped as they got out and paid the driver.

"You ain't seen nuthin' yet, Miss," he said. "Wait'll you try to get in!"

The streets were flooded with a surging, boisterous sea of humanity. Policemen struggled to keep order, while vendors hawked their wares from the curb or mingled with the crowd, peddling T-shirts, programs, posters, photos, lapel pins, dolls, and a variety of other souvenirs.

Amazingly, everyone was in good humor. Even

27

back in placid River Heights, Nancy would have expected an occasional outburst of temper from an overflow crowd. But here the rock fans seemed as patient and cheerful as if they were all old friends.

Patience was certainly needed. The lines inched their way into the auditorium as attendants stationed at half a dozen points checked tickets.

For the first time since receiving the complimentary tickets, Nancy had time to think about what they implied. The eager, keyed-up fans all around her showed how much excitement Lance Warrick and his group generated. The rock king was besieged by girls whenever he appeared in public.

Was it really possible that she had attracted the star's interest just by their brief encounter at the garden party? The thought was certainly flattering!

An Australian backup group, the Didgeridoo, performed first to warm up the audience. Not that any warmup was needed. When the curtains finally rose on the Crowned Heads amid a blaze of psychedelic strobe lights, the whole auditorium seemed to explode!

The storm of applause sank to a pregnant hush as the music came on with a soul-haunted beat. Lance seemed content at first to stand in one spot and pluck his guitar delicately, as though deep in meditation.

But gradually he began to slink back and forth across the stage, twanging more insistently, putting a harder, funkier edge on the music. He was dressed like a futuristic highwayman, in a cocked hat and glittering blue metallic tights, with pistol bandoliers across his bare chest and his legs encased in silver boots.

Sweat beaded his forehead as the music grew louder and his voice rose to a hoarse shout. At times he seemed to be threatening or sneering at the audience, at others, cajoling or making love to it.

When not playing his guitar or taking a quick turn at the synthesizer, he would clutch a portable mike with manic intensity and yell out fresh choruses, all the while prancing, stomping or pirouetting about the stage, occasionally leaping and twirling high in the air.

Barely ten minutes into the concert, the audience was clapping and stamping its feet. And the Crowned Heads gave them no chance to relax. They segued from number to number with scarcely a pause.

But it was Lance Warrick who held the audience mesmerized. He seemed to play on his fans' emotions as easily as he twanged out chords on his guitar. At times Nancy felt certain he was playing and singing especially to *her*.

From the corner of her eye, she stole a swift glance at her girl friends. Both Bess and George were staring at the rock king entranced, their eyes wide open, lips slightly parted.

With a shock, Nancy realized that she had been doing the same thing herself!

Snap out of it! she chided herself jokingly. The guy's a mere human. He's just putting on a show.

But what a show! Dazzling costume changes—highwayman to Indian chief to starship trooper to medieval troubadour—combined with special effects left the audience gasping. Camera crews could be seen taping the show for a rock video.

By the time the curtain descended, Nancy felt exhausted. So, she could see, did Bess and George.

"Well, how did you like it?" she asked.

"I'll never forget tonight!" Bess confided huskily, reaching over to clutch Nancy's hand. All George could do was nod in enthusiastic agreement.

A buzz of chatter filled the auditorium as everyone stood or shifted position to ease their cramped muscles. Some were hurrying up the aisles to the restrooms or for refreshment refills, but most remained seated, knowing the group would soon return for their encore numbers.

A uniformed usher was making his way along the front row. Nancy suddenly realized he was approaching *her*.

"Miss Nancy Drew?"

"Yes . . ."

"This is for you!" He held out a folded message.

5

Press Party

Even before she opened the note, Nancy guessed whom it was from. The paper bore the Crowned Heads' insignia, a cartoon of Lance Warrick weighed down by a huge king's crown sagging at a cockeyed angle, with the other members of the group around him wearing only slightly less imposing coronets.

The message was scrawled in purple ink—royal purple—and signed in his usual joking fashion, *L.R.* Nancy knew this stood for *Lancelot Rex.*

Her two friends were staring at her eagerly.

"Tell us!" begged Bess. "Who's it from?"

"As if we can't guess!" said George.

"Lance is inviting us to the press party after the show."

A chorus of awed exclamations made Nancy

31

aware that her two chums weren't the only ones around her keenly interested in her message from the rock king.

Presently the curtains rose again to loud stamping, cheering and applause as the Crowned Heads returned for their encore. The rock king and his group wound up their performance at peak power, knowing they had their fans completely enthralled.

Nancy felt sure now that it hadn't been just her imagination . . . all those times when he'd paused at the edge of the stage and gazed down through the glare of the spotlights, he really *had* been singing to her! And now he was doing it again!

She shivered with suppressed excitement. How in the world had all this come about? In little more than twenty-four hours, she had not only met the hottest star on the international rock scene, but the acquaintance seemed to be taking a romantic turn!

Let's not get silly now, Nancy cautioned herself. I come from a nice little suburban community called River Heights, and I have a boyfriend back there named Ned Nickerson, who's much more my type than this British wild man, Lance Warrick!

But it was hard to think sensibly with that pulsating rock beat throbbing through the auditorium.

After numerous curtain calls, the show was finally over. The fans began surging out through the aisles as noisily and good-naturedly as they had entered.

"Where exactly is this press party?" inquired George, her mouth close to Nancy's ear.

"The note said any guard could direct us!"

From a transverse aisle behind the orchestra seats, steps led down to a corridor. It, too, was filled with a jostling crowd. But after Nancy displayed her invitation from Lance at several checkpoints, the girls succeeded in reaching a pair of double doors, through which at last they gained admission to the press party.

Inside was bedlam. The reception room seemed filled to overflowing. Several TV crews were busy interviewing celebrities and taping the party for the next morning's news show. The guests were milling about, while waiters circulated with trays of refreshments. And somewhere in the room, Nancy imagined, were Lance and the rest of his group, although she couldn't glimpse any of them.

The babble and din were deafening.

"We should've brought earplugs!" joked Bess.

A television reporter thrust a microphone in Nancy's face. "Hey! Aren't you Nancy Drew, the detective?"

She smiled and nodded, slightly embarrassed.

"Have you solved the mystery of why the whole town's going bananas over Lance Warrick and the Crowned Heads?"

"They're very talented musicians."

"Look! There's Adam Muir!" exclaimed George. He was one of the two group members who had accompanied Lance to the garden party.

A strikingly attractive young woman of twenty-

33

one or twenty-two suddenly loomed at Nancy's shoulder. "Can I help you, luv?" she chirped in a charming British accent. Less charming was her artificial smile.

"I'm Nancy Drew, and these are my two friends, Bess Marvin and George Fayne."

"Is Lance or one of the group expecting you young ladies?" she asked pointedly.

Her face was beautifully painted, and her taffy-blond hair was in an artfully styled bush. Her sleek figure was sheathed in a silver lamé jumpsuit, and on her feet were raspberry suede boots with stiletto heels.

Nancy displayed the handwritten invitation.

"Oh yes, you're *that* one." Her dazzling smile flashed on and off. "Well, Lance may be tied up for a while, but if you'd care to join the other girls . . ."

She fluttered her hand vaguely in the direction of several obvious groupies.

"Thanks, we'll manage."

"Yes, do. And enjoy yourselves. I'm Jane Royce, by the way."

"Do you believe that?" George blurted as the high-styled Miss Royce snaked off through the crowd, hips aswing. She was already beaming her charm at a bald-headed record company executive.

Nancy grinned. "A breath of London in the outposts of empire!"

She had just glimpsed Lance Warrick surrounded

34

by reporters and hangers-on. Would she even have a chance to talk to him in this madhouse?

Bess wormed her way to a refreshment table and returned clutching three glasses. "Two Cokes and one bitter lemon—best I could do!"

She spoke with her mouth half full. After chewing and swallowing hastily, Bess added, "And they have all sorts of yummy-looking tidbits! Let's nibble!"

"You're on a diet, cuddles—remember?" George said sternly.

The swirling tide of the guest throng brought them in sight of the Crowned Heads' drummer, Bobo Evans. Seeing the girls, he plowed a path toward them, accompanied by the synthesizer keyboardist, Adam Muir. Both, like Lance, were still in makeup.

Bobo's moon face was wreathed in a smile. "Blimey, if it ain't the three little dolly-birds from the garden party!" he exclaimed. "You remember that society bash on Long Island, don't you, Adam?"

"But of course, my dear! How could I forget?" The keyboardist's long, delicate fingers brushed Nancy lightly under the chin. "Lancelot was chatting up this lovely little redhead. And thanks to her, we were privileged to meet these other two charmers!"

Bobo came from Liverpool and sounded like Ringo Starr, but Adam's accent was South London cockney, spoken in a high-pitched ladylike simper.

Ned would certainly have disapproved of Adam, but Nancy couldn't help smiling at Adam's insouciant showmanship. She half suspected it was a carefully cultivated act à la Boy George. His face was powdered dead white, and his shiny black hair was slicked back in 1920's movie style. A long cigarette holder dangled from one limp-wristed hand.

"We thought the show was wonderful!" Bess gushed. "You really had the audience turned on!"

"Yeah, well, that's what turns *us* on," said Bobo. "All the birds out there in the concert hall listenin' to us and lovin' us!"

"Must you go back to England so soon?"

"That's what the king says, duckie, but if you can talk him out of it . . .!"

As Bess laughed happily, George said to Adam, "Who's that creature in the silver jumpsuit?"

"Jane Royce, you mean?"

"Right. What's her job?"

"Publicity. Does all our advance promotion. Acts as producer, too, for some of our records when Lance doesn't feel like doing it personally."

"So that's it." George shot an acid glance across the room at the silver-suited young Englishwoman. "She came on as if she was the Crowned Heads' housemother and boss-lady."

36

Adam tittered in delight, one hand on his hip. "My dear, you don't know the half of it! She's the Queen Mum herself! Oh yes, indeed—quite the power behind the throne is our Janie!"

Nancy was not exactly pleased to think of Jane Royce having any control over Lance Warrick, but tried not to show it.

Bess headed back to the refreshment table with Bobo. And Adam was accosted by a feature reporter who drew him away to face the lens of a news photographer. Adam insisted on bringing George along on one arm to pose with him.

George balked at first, fearing she might, in her own words, "look silly." But Adam smoothly overrode her reluctance. Nancy was glad to be left alone to relax and collect her thoughts.

The respite was brief. Feeling a hand on her arm, Nancy turned—and caught her breath as she found herself face to face with Lance Warrick! Her heart gave a sudden lurch.

"Nancy, my sweet! What a charge I got out of seeing you down there in the front row! A vision of loveliness with those red-gold locks!"

It was hard not to smile with pleasure at such words. He went on, "And what a gorgeous surprise! Positively lifted my performance to new heights! I'd no idea you were a rock fan, much less a fan of mine, especially after that brush-off you gave me at the garden party!"

Nancy's smile gave way to bewilderment.

"I . . . I don't understand. Didn't you expect me to use those tickets?"

"What tickets?"

"The ones you sent."

"Me?" It was Lance's turn to look blankly bewildered. "I never sent you any tickets . . ."

6

Powder Bag

Seeing the startled, dismayed expression that flickered over Nancy's face, the rock star groped for a way out.

"Well now, look, luv! The gang all knew what a terrific impression you made on me. I reckon one of them sent you the tickets."

Nancy smiled politely, appreciating his tact. "Yes, I expect it was something like that. . . . Anyhow, I thought your performance tonight was out of this world! You and your group were terrific!"

"I say! Aren't you the sweet thing to shower us with such compliments!"

Nancy felt like falling through the floor. How could she have been so vain as to think a world-famous star like Lance Warrick would go out of his way to invite her to his sell-out concert?!—as his personal guest yet!

Most humiliating of all, she'd exposed her nitwit fantasies! And now he had obviously sized her up as one more groupie candidate . . .

"This press party's just for the vulgar mob," Lance was saying, "but we've laid on a *real* celebration later on at the hotel. Your presence is expected, need I add—by royal command!"

The king of rock slipped a cozy arm around Nancy's waist. "There're a couple of limos standing by. The gang and I'll sneak away as soon as the streets clear a bit and this lot here gets enough of a buzz on so they won't notice. Meantime, why don't you and your friends stick close to the other birds, so we'll know where to find you when the time comes?!"

Nancy felt slightly sick. Already he was consigning her, Bess and George to the status of royal groupies.

"Thanks, but we really can't stay much longer," she heard herself respond. "We'll probably be flying out of New York tomorrow, so we'd better get our beauty sleep."

"Oh, come on now!" Lance wheedled. "What does a ravishing creature like you need with any beauty sleep?"

But Nancy merely smiled and shook her head as she slipped out of his one-armed embrace. He reluctantly let her go with a quick kiss on the cheek as other guests clamored for his attention.

40

Once she was out of Lance's sight, Nancy looked around for a place to collect herself. A powder room offered the nearest refuge. As she hurried toward it, she felt her cheeks burning with shame and tears prickling her eyes.

Fortunately no one seemed to notice her unnerved state. All the other females in the powder room were too busy chattering away excitedly. Nancy found a place in front of the mirror and dashed cold water on her face.

How silly to get upset! she scolded herself. I'll never see Lance again after tonight anyway, so what difference does it make?

She repaired her makeup deftly with a few quick strokes of mascara and dabs of eye shadow and lip gloss. As Nancy turned from the mirror to put the cosmetics in her bag, she caught a fleeting glimpse of a silver-clad figure disappearing out the door.

A faint resentment stirred at the thought that Jane Royce might have observed her distress. But Nancy had her feelings under control now and dismissed the matter with a shrug.

Outside the powder room, the press party was still in full swing.

A magazine writer recognized the famous young sleuth and waylaid her for an interview. While they chatted, Nancy's roving glance spotted George Fayne. She was engaged in a lively discussion with

41

several other guests on the subject, Nancy later learned, of rock music trends.

George rejoined her when the interview was over. Together they went looking for Bess and found her still at the refreshment table. Bobo Evans, it seemed, had wandered off with the group's bass player, Freddie Isham, but Bess had lingered to sample some chocolate strawberries which had just been added to the array of tidbits.

"Heavens, can't we leave you alone for two minutes?" George teased. The complaint ended in a gulp of delight as Bess silenced her by popping one of the strawberries into George's mouth.

"No more! You've had enough!" Bess declared sharply, rapping George's knuckles as her cousin reached for a second helping.

Nancy doubled up with laughter.

"By the way, didn't I see you with Lance War-rick?" Bess asked her titian-haired chum.

"You did. And he invited us to a private party at his hotel. But don't get all atwitter, Bess dear. We're not going," Nancy added, seeing her friend's china-blue eyes light up at the prospect.

Bess's plumply pretty face fell. "Why not?"

"Because he already has us classified as groupie recruits, that's why."

Much of the fun seemed to go out of the party at Nancy's revelation and, as midnight was fast approaching, the three girls decided to leave.

Half an hour later, a taxi deposited them outside the Gothic apartment building on the West Side.

"Hope we won't have to wake your aunt," said George. "Or will she be waiting up?"

"Probably. Aunt Eloise is sort of a night owl. But it doesn't matter either way," said Nancy, rummaging in her handbag. "I have a key."

Suddenly she caught her breath and her hand seemed to freeze. Then she fished out her key and hastily closed her bag.

"Something wrong?" asked Bess.

"Yes, but let's not talk about it now. It's nothing to lose any sleep over. I'll explain tomorrow morning."

After breakfast the next day, George brought up the subject. "Are you going to tell us now what you found in your purse last night, Nan?"

The teenage sleuth nodded and rose from the table. The others followed her into the sitting room. Nancy picked up her handbag, opened it and took out a small transparent plastic bag filled with sparkling white powder.

George's and Bess's eyes widened, and Miss Drew gasped in dismay. "Oh no! Is that what I think it is, Nancy?"

"I'm afraid so, Aunt Eloise. But not to worry. I'll see that it's disposed of properly. Do you mind if a policeman comes here to the apartment?"

"Of course not, my dear. Do as you think best."

Nancy telephoned a lieutenant in the New York

Police Department whom she had met on an earlier case. After hearing her story, he promised to send a narcotics squad detective over.

Later the phone rang. Mrs. Harwood was on the line.

"Nancy dear, you're booked on a flight to London leaving tomorrow evening. Is that agreeable?"

"Wonderful!" Nancy enthused. "Where shall I pick up my ticket? At the airport?"

"You can pick it up this afternoon. My travel agent's holding it for you, along with enough traveler's checks to cover all expenses. Her office is on Fifth Avenue." Mrs. Harwood gave her the exact address, then asked, "What about your passport, dear?"

"No problem. I brought it with me to New York. Daddy was expecting to fly to Venice on legal business and thought I might like to go along, but that's been put on hold. I'm all set."

Bess and George had overheard enough to guess that Nancy's travel arrangements to London had been finalized. Both clamored for details, and Nancy found herself wishing her two girl friends could accompany her on the flight to England.

They were equally wistful. "Gee, wouldn't it be great if we could shop at the London stores together, and take in a concert at the Palladium!" said George.

"Instead of which, we'll be flying home to River Heights," said Bess regretfully.

"Never mind, maybe we can make it a threesome next summer," Nancy said hopefully.

Their chat was interrupted by the bell from the lobby. The police officer had arrived. Nancy buzzed him in, then opened the door to meet him when he stepped off the elevator. He strode toward her down the hall, a sharp-featured, steely-eyed man in plain clothes.

"Sergeant Weintraub, narcotics squad."

"I'm Nancy Drew, Sergeant. Please come in."

She introduced him to her aunt and friends, and invited him to sit down. "I suppose you've been told why I called?" she said to him.

"Only briefly. I'd like to hear it in your own words, Miss Drew."

Nancy explained how she had found the plastic bag full of white powder in her handbag after returning from the concert. "I assume this is cocaine, or am I jumping to conclusions?"

He examined the evidence. "Nope, it's coke, all right—high grade stuff from the looks of it. Any idea how this got in your purse, Miss Drew?"

"Someone put it there, obviously."

"But you've no idea who?"

Nancy hesitated a fraction of a moment. "Not really. I suppose it could've been almost anyone we passed in the street or at the concert."

Weintraub looked dubious. "People don't usually give this stuff away. Once it's cut and sold, this much alone could bring several thousand dollars."

"Or several years in prison, I imagine," Nancy said wryly, "which might be a good reason for getting rid of it in a hurry."

The detective nodded. "Yeah, that figures. Maybe someone had to ditch it fast, and your handbag was the nearest convenient place. At this press party for the Crowned Heads that you went to, did you see anyone handle your purse?"

Nancy thought of the silver-clad figure she'd glimpsed leaving the powder room. "No, but that's not saying it couldn't have happened."

"How well do you know the Crowned Heads?"

The titian-haired teenager shrugged. "Not very. We just met them at a garden party on Long Island two days ago."

"And on the strength of that, you attended their press party last night?"

"Lance Warrick saw us in the audience and had one of the ushers bring us an invitation."

Sergeant Weintraub frowned thoughtfully. "He didn't by any chance invite you to the private party later on at his hotel?"

"As a matter of fact he did, during the press reception. But it was already getting close to midnight and, well, we thought it best to come on home."

"Smart girl!"

Nancy shot the narcotics officer a cool glance. "What exactly are you implying?"

46

"It so happens we got an anonymous phone tip saying there'd be drugs at that party."

Nancy was startled, as the significance of his remark flashed through her mind. "You don't mean you *raided* the Crowned Heads' hotel suite?"

Weintraub nodded emphatically. "We sure did, with a search warrant. If you'd been there with that bag of cocaine in your purse, you'd probably be behind bars right now, Miss Drew!"

7

Surprise Meeting

Timing, thought Nancy, was everything. Later she wondered how differently her whole adventure in England might have turned out if she hadn't chanced to pass that particular door at Heathrow Airport at that particular moment.

Her transatlantic flight had been smooth and uneventful. She had read *Wicca: The Way of Wisdom* until she dozed off around 11:00 P.M. When she awoke, daylight was seeping in the curtained window, and the thought uppermost in her mind was Sergeant Weintraub's remark about the bag of cocaine that someone had slipped into her handbag.

Had someone deliberately tried to bring about her arrest on a narcotics charge?

Her musing ended when the stewardesses served breakfast. Nancy dismissed the unpleasant subject

from her mind as she ate and chatted with the
Japanese electronics salesman sitting next to her.
Presently the pilot announced over the intercom
that the plane was approaching London. Twenty
minutes later the passengers were disembarking
into Terminal 3.

Heathrow struck Nancy as the biggest, busiest,
most confusing, most sprawling airport she had ever
passed through. There seemed to be a large number
of young people and news cameramen everywhere
she looked. The corridors seemed interminable,
and one of the moving walkways had broken down.
But the passport inspection was conducted with
typical British courtesy, and her luggage was simply
waved through Her Majesty's Customs with a
cheery smile of welcome.

Nancy was pushing a cart through what she
hoped was the final corridor leading to the terminal
exit when a voice called out, "'Oi there, Red!"

No one at home ever called her that—her hair
shone too lustrously golden for such a monochro-
matic nickname. Besides, why would any cockney
be hailing Nancy Drew?

Curiosity turned her head, nevertheless. A door
had just opened and a face was grinning out at her
from a room off the corridor. It was Freddie Isham,
the Crowned Heads' bass player!

"Stone the crows! Wotcher doin' 'ere in England,
luvvie?"

Freddie was a jolly, hulking teddy bear with a

swarthy touch of West Indian blood, easily the most good-natured and likeable of the group.

"Just landed, what does it look like?" Nancy grinned back, pointing to her luggage cart.

Freddie reached his big paw out to draw her into the room. "I was 'avin' a dekko for our chauffeur, and look 'oo turned up!" he announced proudly.

"Blimey, you must be telepathic!" chortled Bobo Evans. He and Adam Muir enthusiastically welcomed the American teenager.

The room seemed full of helmeted policemen. They were obviously preparing to buck the crowd of fans and escort the Crowned Heads out of the terminal as soon as their limousine was in position at the door. Nancy suddenly understood why she had seen all those young people and news cameramen drifting so expectantly about the airport.

Then her eyes fell on Lance Warrick—and her heart flipped. There was no mistaking the glint in his eyes. He wasn't just turning on the charm for another groupie, he was genuinely delighted to see her!

"Nancy, me ould luv!" he cried, and pushed past several bobbies to enfold her in his arms.

"Whoa—hey!" Turning her cheek to his kiss, she laughingly disengaged from his embrace. But there was no mistaking the effect on her pulse.

Over Lance's shoulder, Nancy glimpsed a look of vexation on Jane Royce's stylishly pretty face.

"Don't tell me someone's meeting you?" said

Lance. "Never mind. If there is, the poor chump's out of luck! You're riding into town with us!"

Soon they were speeding along the left-hand side of the highway toward central London in a limousine long and glossy enough for the Royal Family.

Lance had a townhouse in Chelsea and wanted Nancy to be his guest. But she insisted on taking the room Mrs. Harwood had booked for her at Claridge's Hotel in the snazzy Mayfair district of London's West End.

"All right, my pet. But you're lunching with me, and let's have no backchat!"

"But Lance darling, you have all sorts of press interviews set up for this afternoon," wailed Jane Royce. "And I've laid on a business meeting with the record company about your next video."

"So plead jet lag and reschedule." Turning to the American girl, he went on, "One o'clock sharp, then, right luv?"

Nancy smiled as the Claridge's doorman held open the door of the limousine for her. "Well . . . okay, since you're twisting my arm!"

At the reception desk, a frock-coated hotel clerk informed Nancy that she'd had a phone call less than half an hour ago from Lady Lisa Penvellyn.

"This is her number, Miss Drew. She asked if you'd ring her up as soon as you arrived."

"Thank you."

Lisa was ecstatic. "Oh Nancy, how good it is to hear your voice!"

51

"And yours, Lisa!"

"I can't tell you how much I look forward to talking over old times. I've been counting the hours ever since Mom told me you were coming! How soon can you start for Cornwall?"

Nancy had been prepared to leave London that afternoon after a brief rest and change of clothes. But her unexpected lunch date and a chance to see more of Lance Warrick had suddenly scrambled her plans. "Well, how about tomorrow, Lisa?"

"Oh, good! I'll count on that, Nan! Let me tell you how to get here. Penvellyn Castle's located just outside a little fishing village called Polpenny on the south coast of Cornwall. You can get an express train out of Paddington Station that'll—"

"Whoa—let me get a pencil!" laughed Nancy.

After she hung up, she showered and changed into a smart green and white striped silk dress, to which she added a straw hat. When Lance phoned from the lobby, she was ready.

He was hiding behind dark glasses, but they still had to make a run for it from the hotel to evade a sudden deluge of screeching rock fans. Nancy couldn't help feeling elated as they zoomed off in his sleek, open red sports car, which a bellhop had been holding ready with its engine running.

She was also touched and pleased when Lance insisted on giving her a quick guided tour through the heart of London before lunch.

What a feast it all is, thought Nancy. The bustling

pageant of Picadilly Circus and Trafalgar Square with its column and lions, a glimpse of the scarlet-plumed Horse Guards at Whitehall, then up Fleet Street, with the dome of St. Paul's floating on the skyline, toward the fabled Tower of London and Tower Bridge.

Lance circled back north past the British Museum. Then he turned south again through Soho toward the Thames to take in the Houses of Parliament as Big Ben was striking the quarter-hour, and historic Westminster Abbey, followed by the climactic spectacle of Buckingham Palace, with a brace of bearskinned, red-coated Grenadier Guards on sentry duty.

Nancy had seen it all before, but she loved seeing it again.

The gray, stately old city with its lovely green parks was changing. There were more modern towers and office blocks amid the ancient landmarks than Nancy had noticed on her last trip.

And the clothing styles were certainly changing, too! The streets teemed with young people in the wildest imaginable outfits. Cross-gender dressing, bizarre haircuts and hairdos—everyone seemed bent on achieving the most outrageous possible image.

"They make me feel positively stodgy!" Nancy smiled.

Lance beamed at her admiringly. "Ah, but there's one important difference you're forgetting!"

"What's that?"

"None of those dolly-birds is as lovely as you!"

Crossing Sloane Square, they drove west down King's Road through trendy Chelsea. Lance sped on past the urban sprawl to a quiet pub with garden tables overlooking the river.

As they lunched on salad, prawns and quiche, Nancy found herself forgetting that she was the guest of a famous rock star. Aside from his accent, she might have been chatting with a young American she'd known from high school.

But his background was certainly worlds different from Ned Nickerson's. Workingclass by birth, Lance Warrick had made it to Oxford on brains alone. Originally he'd planned to be a serious composer.

"What made you turn to rock?" she inquired.

Lance grinned sharply. "Ambition. I reckoned that was the fastest way to open doors and make meself rich and famous."

As he spoke, his voice lost some of its Oxford accent and reverted to that of a Midland factory town. It also took on a slight edge.

"I'm not sure I believe that," Nancy said quietly.

"You'd better, luv. It's the truth. Beethoven was a rare old hand at crankin' out symphonies, but he'd have a rough time gettin' one played today, especially if he came from Leeds or Birmingham."

"Symphonies aren't the only kind of music worth

hearing. I'll admit I'm no expert, but I've been listening to your group ever since you first began making records. You started out as a mix of punk and heavy metal, and then got more and more new wave and progressive. But right now there isn't *any* label that fits. Your music is different from anything else on the rock scene today. What makes you so sure the London Symphony or New York Philharmonic *won't* be playing it some day?"

Lance Warrick looked into her eyes for a long moment. Then he murmured, "You're quite an interesting woman, aren't you, Nancy Drew?"

A feminine figure was coming across the garden. The spell that had woven itself around her and Lance was suddenly broken as Nancy recognized Jane Royce.

"I do hate to interrupt this cozy little twosome," the English girl said, "but I'm afraid we have an urgent problem with Ian Purcell, Lance."

"Ian?" The rock star frowned at her irritably. "He's still sunning himself in Polpenny, isn't he?"

"Not any more. He's back in London, and acting very oddly, it appears."

"What's that supposed to mean?"

Jane Royce shrugged a shapely shoulder. "Dunno, darling. I couldn't quite make it all out over the phone, but his landlady's threatening to call the police unless you come round straightaway."

Lance flung down his napkin angrily. "What a freaking bore!" To Nancy he added, "Could you possibly forgive me if I—"

She smiled. "Don't apologize, I understand. Ian Purcell used to be your bass player, didn't he?"

"That's right, till he got on drugs."

"And he's just back from Polpenny, in Cornwall?"

Lance nodded, intrigued by her question.

"Then if I may," said Nancy, "I'll come with you."

8

An Unexpected Visitor

"What, may one ask, is so important about Polpenny?" asked Jane Royce as they drove back into London.

Her taxi to the pub had been dismissed, and she was crammed, none too happily, into the tiny back seat of Lance's red sports car.

"I've been invited to visit there," said Nancy. She told how her friend had married Lord Penvellyn.

"I'm not sure I get the connection, darling. I mean, what does the fact that Ian's been loafing around Polpenny while he gets his head together, have to do with your friend in Penvellyn Castle?"

Nancy chose to shrug lightly. "If he knows Polpenny, perhaps he can tell me what it's like."

"From the way his landlady sounded, I doubt if Ian's in any state to tell anybody anything."

Nancy made no reply. The notion that Ian Purcell's strange behavior might be related to Lisa Penvellyn's mysterious trouble seemed far-fetched. Nevertheless, the double connection with Polpenny seemed an odd coincidence, and Nancy was determined to find out more.

Purcell, it turned out, had rooms in a part of the city called Holland Park, which he used on trips back to London while recovering from his drug addiction in Cornwall.

His lodging house, not far off Kensington High Street, was a once imposing stucco villa with a pillared porch that lent it a touch of faded grandeur. Now grimy with age, it looked like a dignified old woman who had sunk into genteel poverty.

"Oh, Mr. Warrick!" the landlady clucked. "I've been trying to reach you ever since I heard on the telly that you were back. A girl at one of the record studios finally told me where to call, after I explained it was about Mr. Purcell."

"What exactly is wrong with him, Mrs. Roby?"

"Oh dear, it'll break your heart when you see him, Mr. Warrick! He's hardly moved or said a word since he got in early yesterday, and when he does talk, it's just gibberish. A gentleman who came to see him this morning couldn't get any sense out of him, either."

"Sounds like he's coming down from a bad drug trip," Lance muttered to Jane as they followed the landlady up the stairs.

58

"Oh no, he's been staying off drugs, that I do believe!" put in Mrs. Roby. "If he hadn't, you can be sure I'd have sent him packing."

She knocked on the door of her lodger's room. When there was no response, Lance opened it, only to stop short with a stifled exclamation.

Ian Purcell, Nancy now saw, occupied a dingy but spacious one-room apartment furnished in florid Victorian style. He was seated in front of the fireplace partially facing the door. The skinny, straw-haired bass player showed only the barest awareness of his visitors. His eyes seemed haunted and his mouth hung open with a trace of drool from one corner.

"For God's sake, Ian, snap out of it!" Lance blurted. But the rocker's sole response when shaken was a babble of meaningless sounds.

"How long has he been like this, Mrs. Roby?"

"A good day and a half, it's been. 'Twasn't six A.M. when he got in yesterday. Cook was in the kitchen when she heard him at the door. He had a key, of course, but couldn't fit it in the lock, so he rang the bell. When she let him in, he collapsed in her arms. She had to wake our handyman, and the two of them got him upstairs to his room. Since then, I've heard him stumbling about a bit now and then, but that's all."

Lance Warrick heaved a heavy sigh. "All right, I suppose we'd better call an ambulance."

Nancy spoke diffidently to the landlady, "Did you say Mr. Purcell had a visitor this morning?"

"That's right, Miss. Quite a nice-dressed gentleman, he was."

"Did he give his name?"

"Hmm, seems he did, but I don't recall offhand. Some kind of art dealer, I believe. Wait now—he left a card, come to think of it."

While Lance went to phone for an ambulance, Mrs. Roby fetched the card to show Nancy. It named the caller as Eustace Thorne, a dealer in objets d'art with a shop on Pimlico Road.

Lance soon returned from the telephone. He decided that he and Jane Royce would ride along with the ambulance to inspect the sanatorium where Ian would be taken and arrange for the best possible medical care. "In the meantime, Nancy, you can drive my car back to your hotel," he said. "Jane can pick it up later. Better yet, I'll pick it up myself when I come to take you out to dinner tonight!"

"We're dining, are we?" Nancy smiled quizzically.

"Of course we are—to make up for the way our lunch was cut short!"

"All right. But are you sure you want me operating that beautiful machine in London traffic? I've never driven on the left-hand side of the street before."

"Nothing to it, luv. I'll show you the controls myself."

Before leaving, Nancy said she wanted to talk to the art dealer who had visited Ian Purcell. Lance told her how to get to Pimlico. "It's right between Buckingham Palace and Chelsea. We passed it."

It was a thrill driving the lovely red sports car through London. Pimlico, Lance had informed her, was a newly fashionable shopping area.

Eustace Thorne, a silk-suited man with a walrus mustache and a carnation in his lapel, was more than willing to answer Nancy's questions. Lance Warrick, she learned, had phoned ahead to introduce her.

"May I ask why you went to see Ian Purcell, Mr. Thorne?" she began.

"About the Golden Mab, my dear. You see, he told me last week that he'd recently seen a duplicate of the statuette."

"The Golden Mab?" Nancy Drew frowned. "Should I know what that means?"

The art dealer shrugged and fluttered his well-manicured hands. "Perhaps not, if you've just arrived in London. It's been receiving a good deal of media coverage lately. The statuette is a bust of the old pagan British goddess Mab, or Maeve, as the Irish call her. She's sometimes known as the Goddess of the Witches."

61

Witches! Another coincidence? Nancy repressed a shiver of excitement as Eustace Thorne went on. "It's the finest example of ancient Celtic art ever discovered. It's now on display at the Tate Gallery, by courtesy of the present owner, to whom I sold the bust last year."

"It's quite valuable then?"

"The gold alone makes it worth a small fortune. As an historical art treasure, ten times its weight in gold would be a modest valuation."

Nancy regarded Thorne thoughtfully. "You believe Ian Purcell was telling the truth?"

"Who knows, my dear? All I can tell you is that art experts have traditionally held that the Golden Mab was one of a matching pair. A layman like Purcell would be unlikely to know that. Yet he told me this other Mab he'd seen faced right, whereas the bust at the Tate Gallery faces left. It gave his story a certain ring of authenticity."

"Did he give you any hint where he'd seen this other Mab?"

Eustace Thorne shook his head sadly. "Alas, no. He merely left his name and address, and promised to return with photographic evidence. When he failed to do so, I took it upon myself to pay him a visit. I gather you saw with your own eyes the condition I found him in."

When Nancy arrived back at Claridge's, she decided this would be a good time to phone her father. With the five-hour time difference between

London and River Heights, he should be breaking for lunch soon.

Carson Drew's delight upon hearing from his daughter was evident even over three thousand miles of ocean. "How are things in jolly old London, honey?"

"Marvelous, Daddy! I'm having such fun! I haven't even seen Lisa yet, but I've already stumbled on a brand new mystery."

"That's no surprise, coming from my favorite sleuth. By the way, let me give you the name and number of a law firm you can go to if you run into any complications. It's Huntley & Dawlish, in Lincoln's Inn. They're top-flight criminal barristers. They can advise you, or put you in touch with the right man at Scotland Yard."

"Oh, good!" Nancy wrote down the information.

Her father also reported that there was a special clause in Lisa's trust fund that provided for Mrs. Harwood to serve as executor should her daughter ever become ill or incompetent.

Nancy had barely hung up when the phone rang. She felt a moment's panic—surely this couldn't be Lance Warrick so early. She hadn't even changed or showered yet!

Instead, a hotel clerk's voice informed her that a Miss Jane Royce was in the lobby.

"Oh yes, of course. Ask her to come up, please."

The young Englishwoman wore a cool smile when Nancy opened the door to her knock.

"Surprised to see me?"

"Not at all. Do come in. I'm sorry I have no refreshments to offer you, but let me call—"

"No, no. I can't stay long, darling, so let me get right to the point."

Jane Royce took a chair and helped herself to a cigarette before speaking. "You're rather fond of Lance, aren't you?"

"He's certainly been very nice to me," Nancy replied, "and I'm sure any girl would call him attractive. Yes, I do like him."

Her visitor's smile became a trifle patronizing. "I thought so. Well, Nancy dear, may I offer a word of advice?"

"Of course."

"Don't get *too* fond of him."

"Why not?"

"We haven't broken the news yet, even to the rest of the group, but you see, Lance and I plan to marry soon."

9

A Night on the Town

Though taken aback and hurt by the news, Nancy forced a smile and murmured, "Congratulations."

"One congratulates the man, dear," Jane Royce responded, "and wishes the bride-to-be happiness."

"You're right, of course, Jane. I spoke without thinking. And I do wish you every happiness."

"How sweet! You're not offended, I hope, at my saying all this?"

"Not at all." Nancy found it hard to go on smiling, but did her best to inject some warmth into her voice. "I appreciate your frankness. In your place, I would have done the same thing."

"Good! Then I needn't take up any more of your time." The taffy-blond Londoner rose with feline grace and stubbed out her cigarette in a hotel ashtray. "Lance will still come round to take you out to dine—with my blessings," she added silkily, "so enjoy yourself, darling!"

She was gone before the American girl could fully collect herself and recover her emotional poise.

Alone once again, Nancy bit her lip to keep it from quivering, but she could feel tears welling in her eyes. How could Lance have been so insensitive! Leading her on and watching her respond to his flirtatious advances, while all the while his fiancée looked on, pitying her naivete!

She felt like flinging herself on the bed and sobbing. But Nancy had never been one to indulge in self-pity. Instead, she concentrated on filing her nails, until her feelings calmed down. Then she dashed off a letter to Hannah Gruen and prepared to shower.

By the time Lance arrived, she had changed into a sapphire-blue dress which reflected her sapphire eyes and set off her red-gold hair perfectly. Around her neck was a small string of pearls which, with matching earrings, had been her eighteenth birthday present from Carson Drew.

The result was obvious from Lance's expression. "Did anyone ever tell you you're beautiful?" he said huskily, offering his arm.

Nancy dimpled. "Well, let's see now. Yes, I seem to recall hearing that line a few times—from my boyfriend back in the States."

"He must be some kind of dork then, if it's just a line. You're flat-out gorgeous, luv!"

They dined at Suzabelle's in Curzon Street. The decor was campily 1950's with posters and newspaper blowups on the walls from that era. The atmosphere was one of balloons-and-confetti, and Rock King Lance Warrick was plainly a favorite patron. They were showered with attention, and their table was beset by eager fans until the maîtred' took up the microphone and forbade further autograph-hunting.

Nancy found her spirits lifting. Over dessert and coffee, Lance said, "This Yank boyfriend you were telling me about, is it serious?"

"We haven't decided yet."

"Then it's not."

Nancy smiled. "I didn't say that. Ned and I've been going together so long we found ourselves taking each other for granted. So we decided to date other people till we make up our minds."

"Wise child. I'll drink to that!"

"What about yourself?" said Nancy. "I understand congratulations are in order for you and Jane."

Lance set down his cup. "Now what scheming little birdie told you that tiresome twaddle? Dear little Janie Royce, no doubt?"

Nancy shrugged evasively. "Does it matter?"

"Yes, it ruddy well does! Let me tell you something, my sweet. Janie's been at me since the Year One to go tripping down the aisle with her, and I just keep telling her to belt-up. I wouldn't take that kind of nonsense from any other bird. The thing is, she's good at her job—too good to sack."

Lance paused with a look of embarrassment and twiddled the stem of his glass reflectively. "Oh, we've had our tender moments, Janie and I, if you must know . . . but that's *all* they were—just the odd kiss and hug at times when we've both been under pressure or just launched a new record successfully. What matters is that Jane's the best in the business when it comes to publicity. Got a sixth sense for what'll make the headlines, that girl. She knows how to squeeze every drop of favorable press coverage out of any angle that comes along! Do you understand what I'm trying to say, luv?"

Nancy's eyes glowed back at him. She was suddenly feeling much happier. "Yes, I think so."

"Good! Then let's get on with the evening!"

The evening was indeed just beginning. From the restaurant, they drove to The Camden Palace in North London. "Best club in Europe!" Lance confided to her at the door.

The music level inside blasted her ears, and the costumes of the patrons were the most bizarre that Nancy had seen yet.

Afterward they went to two of London's avant-garde nomadic clubs, which Lance told her did not even advertise and had no fixed address. "Très exclusive!" he chuckled. "One only gets to know where they are by word of mouth."

Nancy could believe it. One of the clubs consisted of a tent set up for the night in the empty shell of an abandoned building!

As they danced, Lance whispered in her ear, "You're quite a girl, Nancy Drew! When we first met, even this morning at the airport, I thought you were just an exceptionally lovely bit of crumpet. But you're much more than that, you know. You're something quite special!"

Their lips met . . . tenderly, despite the loud blare of rock music.

"Must you go to Cornwall tomorrow?" Lance asked softly before depositing her at Claridge's later that night.

"I'm afraid I must. I promised my friend—which reminds me, how is Ian Purcell?"

"Still tripping—if that's the explanation."

"How odd," Nancy mused with a puzzled frown. "I wish I *knew* the explanation."

"Look here," said Lance. "If you'll stay on for tomorrow morning, I'll take you to see him, and you can speak to the doctor yourself."

"Hmm, I must admit I'm curious enough to accept your offer, but I'd also like to pay a quick visit to the Tate Gallery."

"Say no more, then. It's a date, darling!"

Next morning, after breakfast at the hotel, they drove to Hampstead, a charming villagelike spot in north London. The clinic to which Ian had been taken was a half-timbered Elizabethan country house overlooking the wild green heath.

69

Dr. Palmer, the white-coated psychiatrist in charge, patiently answered Nancy's questions, but admitted he found the case baffling.

"Could his condition simply be due to an overdose?" Nancy inquired.

Dr. Palmer shook his head. "Most unlikely. In fact, he shows certain physical withdrawal symptoms that indicate he was quitting drugs cold turkey. Emotionally, he behaves as though he's undergone a terrifying shock, some experience which literally scared him out of his wits."

The medic frowned and hesitated. "And there's one other odd circumstance . . ."

"What's that, Doctor?" Nancy asked.

"Mr. Purcell has a needle puncture mark in the back of one leg—not at all a place where I should think it could have been self-inflicted."

"Does that suggest anything?"

Dr. Palmer shrugged uncomfortably. "Perhaps that he was deliberately injected with some mind-scrambling drug that has left him in his present disoriented state. I'm afraid one can only hope that time and rest will restore his full faculties."

Nancy was thoughtful on the ride back into central London. "How did Ian happen to go to Polpenny after he left your group, Lance?"

"Search me. He and Bobo Evan were mates, and they seemed to fancy the place. They'd often go there to unwind between gigs."

The imposing neoclassical Tate Gallery, on an

embankment of the Thames, was their next stop. Nancy was eager to see again the fantastic drawings of William Blake and the glowing watercolors of Joseph Turner. But her favorite of favorites was a wall of Victorian fairy paintings, especially one called *The Fairy Feller's Master Stroke* by a mad English artist, Richard Dadd, who died without explaining his strange masterpiece.

"Blimey, what do you make of that?" said Lance.

"In a word, I think it's wonderful!"

Nancy's main interest that day, however, was the Golden Mab. The bust was displayed amid a variety of modern and abstract sculpture. A placard said that it represented an ancient Celtic fertility goddess and had originally been dug up in the Somerset marshes during the reign of Henry VIII.

The lovely gold statuette portrayed a woman gazing at herself in a mirror.

"Vain old bird, eh?" murmured Lance.

"With much to be vain about," replied Nancy. As the art dealer had said, this Mab held the mirror in her left hand and looked to the left.

There was no time for lunch if Nancy hoped to arrive in Polpenny at a convenient hour. But Lance took her to watch the colorful changing of the guard before driving on to Paddington Station.

"By the way," Lance said with a grin at the last moment, through the window of the train, "I've a surprise announcement to make."

"You'd better make it fast!"

71

A voice was already booming over the PA system that her train was about to depart.

"I'll be seeing you in Cornwall, luv!"

Nancy's heart danced. "In a word—*wonderful!*" She leaned out of the window and blew him a kiss as her train pulled out of the station.

10

A Haunted Land

The train ride to Penzance, which was the nearest station to Polpenny, lasted almost five hours but Nancy enjoyed it thoroughly. She thought she'd never seen a countryside so richly green; and it was somehow comforting to look at.

The train out of London had been crowded with travelers. On the last leg of the journey, however, Nancy found herself alone in the compartment with a tweedy, red-faced old gentleman with a bristly white military mustache and a smelly pipe. But she soon forgave him the pipe as a fair exchange for his interesting conversation.

"Ever been to Cornwall before, young lady?" he inquired with bluff, soldierly directness.

"No, are we close?" Nancy replied.

"That river we just crossed was the Tamar. To a

Cornishman, everyone from the other side of the Tamar, English or not, is a foreigner."

"They sound rather clannish."

The elderly gentleman chuckled. "One could say that. And the attitude's not all one-sided, come to that. There was a time when tots in Devon were told that Cornishmen had tails!"

Nancy laughed appreciatively.

"I'm Colonel Tremayne, by the way. Retired."

"And I'm Nancy Drew."

"American, I take it, from your charming accent?"

"Yes, though opinions differ on our accent, I imagine! And are you Cornish, by any chance?"

"You guessed from my name, no doubt."

"No, should I have?"

"You've not heard the old jingle, then: *By Lan, Ros, Car—Pol, Tre and Pen—ye may know the Cornishmen. . . . Tre* for Tremayne."

Nancy smiled with pleasure. "I find *that* rather charming, Colonel! Thank you for telling me. But why *do* Cornishmen feel so different? Is it just because they live in the farthest west corner of Britain, on their own separate peninsula?"

"Partly that, I dare say. But people also forget that jolly old England's actually a mixture of two hostile races."

"What do you mean?"

"Celts and Anglo-Saxons. The movies, you know,

74

would have us believe that King Arthur and his knights spoke Oxford English, which is nonsense, of course. They were Romanized Celts who spoke old Welsh or Cornish when they weren't talking Latin. The nearest thing to English-speakers in those days were their enemies, the Saxon barbarians from across the Channel. In the end, the two sides got together, but not before the Celts had been overrun and nearly pushed off their own island."

Nancy stared dreamily out the coach window. "How I loved those old stories of King Arthur and his Knights of the Round Table!"

"So did we all, my dear. Some say they're sleeping under a hill, ready to come out and fight again if Britain's ever invaded."

Nancy shivered. "What a thrilling superstition!"

"Perhaps not everyone in these parts would call it a superstition."

"Are you serious?"

Colonel Tremayne shrugged and refilled his pipe gravely. "Let's just say it's a haunted land you've come to, Miss Drew, full of myths and legends."

Nancy was silent a while, thinking of elf-darts and witches and the twin Golden Mab. "Is Cornwall really so ancient?" she asked presently.

"Oldest corner of Britain, my dear. There were Stone Age miners digging tin and copper hereabouts long before Athens and Rome were built. Phoenician traders came here and carried the ore to the Mediterranean. Some say that's why you'll still see a good many dark-haired, hook-nosed Cornish-men."

Nancy glimpsed rocky headlands and blue sea and picturesque fishing villages. At one point she did a startled double take. "Were those *palm trees* I just saw?"

Her companion smiled. "You're on the Cornish Riviera now, my dear. Warming influence of the Gulf Stream. It's another reason tourists flock here, not to mention artists and writers and other such layabouts."

By the time she descended from the train at Penzance, Nancy was eager to see more of Corn-wall. Lisa was waiting to greet her, and the two girls fell into each other's arms.

"Oh, Nancy! You're looking just beautiful!"

"So are you, Lisa." But Nancy secretly crossed her fingers, unhappy at having to fib.

"No, I'm not. You needn't worry about hurting my feelings, Nancy. I see myself in the mirror every morning. To tell the truth, I haven't been feeling well these last few months, but now that you're here, I'm sure I'll perk up."

"Oh, I hope so, Lisa dear!"

In the station parking lot they came to a huge, lemon-colored British roadster of 1920's or 1930's vintage, with a hood that looked about a mile long to Nancy.

"Good night! Is this your royal carriage?"

Lisa giggled. "It belonged to Hugh's uncle, the old Lord Penvellyn from whom he inherited the castle. Uncle Nick was quite a lively old dog. I'm told he bought this dinosaur in his youth, before the Battle of Britain, and loved it so much he kept it in tip-top shape. Hugh considers it the best part of his inheritance!"

Lisa had the porter load Nancy's luggage into the car, and moments later the two girls drove off. Nancy was thrilled as they whizzed along smoothly.

"Your husband's right, Lisa. This car's a gem! I wish Ned could see it!"

"Speaking of whom, how are things between you two, Nancy?"

"We've decided to date other people for a while."

"Ah, so things are at that stage, are they? And do I gather you've already met someone new and interesting? or even fascinating?"

"Well . . ." Nancy smiled somewhat noncommittally. "Interesting, yes. And I guess most girls would call him fascinating, too, but I'm not sure I'm ready to talk about him just yet."

Lisa threw her an understanding smile. "All right, we'll save all that for a cozy chat later."

"What about yourself—you and Hugh, I mean? Are you enjoying the state of holy matrimony?"

Nancy was shocked at the shadow that seemed to fall across her friend's face.

"I love Hugh more than ever, Nancy," Lisa replied in a voice that sounded slightly unsteady, "but I'll admit things haven't been perfect since we settled in at Penvellyn Castle."

"Can I help?" Nancy asked after a pause.

Lisa looked at her. "That's why you're here, isn't it?"

"Yes." Nancy flushed, but decided the truth was preferable to deceit. "That's not the only reason I've come, though. I did want to see you. But your mother was very worried and . . . well, all that seemed a good enough reason."

"I thought so, and I'm glad you've come, Nancy . . . but I'm not sure what you or anyone can do."

"Is there anything you'd care to tell me?"

Her friend shrugged unhappily. "It's all so vague and . . . depressing, I hardly know how to answer that, Nancy. Hardly anyone in Polpenny will even speak to me. It's as if they resent my coming to Penvellyn Castle. And Hugh seems terribly glum and weighed down, as though he's carrying some dreadful secret. And I've been feeling rotten, and—oh dear, nothing seems to have gone right for us!"

Lisa's voice quavered and her eyes glistened.

Nancy patted her hand. "All right . . . you can tell me all about it when we have that cozy chat."

Penzance seemed a colorful, bustling summer resort. But once they were outside the town on the road to Polpenny, the landscape became rugged and stark, and Nancy began to glean a sense of Cornwall as a remote peninsula jutting out into the wild Atlantic.

"I should probably be giving you the standard tourist lecture," said Lisa.

"Never mind," Nancy chuckled. "I've already had one from an old gentleman on the train."

Polpenny actually lay beyond Penvellyn Castle, so Nancy had little chance to take it in before she was overwhelmed by the spectacle of the castle itself. The ancient, mossy stone pile stood on a rugged headland overlooking the sea, just as she had seen it in the photo, with the fishing village a mere cluster of roofs around the harbor at the foot of the grassy slopes of the cove.

"Well?" Lisa smiled as they parked in the courtyard and got out of the car. "How do you like it?"

Nancy stared up at the gray walls, wide-eyed. "I'm breathless!"

"We only live in one wing—oh, here comes Hugh!"

Nancy had met the present Lord Penvellyn at the time of his wedding to Lisa, soon after he inherited the title. Black-haired and in his late twenties, he was a tall, powerfully built young man with a strong jaw and thick dark brows that almost met over a fierce hawk nose. He had been a foreign correspondent, but since his marriage, he had been writing a book on international politics.

Nancy thought that, like Lisa, he looked drawn

and tired. His mood seemed almost somber, though he smiled cordially as he took her hand. "I'm so glad you've come, Nancy. I know how much Lisa's been looking forward to your visit."

"I'm sure it'll be fun for both of us, Hugh!"

Nancy had time to rest and change for dinner, which was served in a high-ceilinged, paneled room, on a large refectory table. The long summer twilight had faded when they finally moved into the drawing room for coffee.

Hugh was telling Nancy about the progress of his book. "It's coming rather slowly, I'm afraid. The world situation's changing so fast th—"

He broke off as a scream suddenly rent the air from the courtyard outside!

11

Spook Attack

Hugh leaped to his feet. "What the deuce was that?!"

"Someone's been hurt!" cried Lisa.

The three ran from the drawing room into the great hall of the castle.

Landreth the butler and one of the maids came rushing into the small anteroom that lay between the great hall and the front door.

"What's happened, Landreth?" Hugh inquired.

"I don't know, m'luv. I'll turn on the ground lights."

The whole courtyard was brightly illumined as they stepped outside, but no one was in sight.

"Perhaps someone's outside the gateway," said the butler after peering around.

He and Hugh hurried to check. Moments later

they returned, supporting a woman between them. She looked close to sixty and was somewhat disheveled, with her broad-brimmed felt hat askew over one eye, but seemed otherwise unhurt.

"Why, it's Ethel Bosinny!" gasped Lisa.

"A friend of yours?" Nancy asked.

"Yes, one of the few I've made in Polpenny! She's a retired games-mistress from a girls' school near here. She instructed the girls in sports there. A bit dotty, but she's been a great comfort to me!"

When Miss Bosinny was seated in the drawing room and given a cup of tea, they learned that she had been bicycling up to the castle gateway when a startling figure loomed out of the darkness.

"Was it anyone you recognized?" Hugh asked.

"I—I really couldn't say." Ethel Bosinny gave a hoarse, embarrassed laugh. "Perhaps it was all my imagination. Anyhow, my bicycle went off the path and turned over, and I lay there stunned until you and Landreth came and helped me up."

She said she had been coming to pay a neighborly call on the Penvellyns, and the village postmistress had asked her to deliver a letter to their young American visitor. Unfortunately, she had dropped it when her bike overturned. Landreth retrieved the bicycle, but neither he nor the maid could find the letter.

Miss Bosinny was much distressed. "Oh my! I'm dreadfully sorry, Miss Drew. I don't know how I could have been so careless!"

"Never mind," Nancy smiled. "I'm sure it'll turn up. It was good of you to bring it."

The next morning Lisa showed Nancy around the castle.

"The original stronghold was built by the Normans back in the twelfth century," she explained. "Most of it has crumbled away, but the central keep has been preserved. Beginning in the 1500's, wings were added, connecting the keep to other buildings inside the bailey, or outer wall. We're living in the newest wing, which I'm told was built in 1650 or thereabouts."

Nancy chuckled. "1650 is close enough for me. I must say, it's withstood the centuries very well."

"We've added a few modern conveniences, of course, like central heating and plumbing."

Nancy was glad to hear her friend laugh. Her visit already seemed to have cheered Lisa up.

The older, unoccupied parts of the castle were now open to public tours. Much of the woodwork in these areas had long ago rotted away, and most of the furnishings, too, had decayed or been removed, leaving little behind but drafty, echoing stone ruins. But as the two friends strolled back to the central keep, Nancy was surprised to see one room shut off by a stout, iron-bound oak door.

"What's in here?" she asked curiously.

"I don't know."

"Aren't you curious?"

Lisa hesitated. Her cheeks seemed to have lost

83

color again. "Hugh keeps that room shut up. I'm not sure why, but he—he seems to feel quite strongly about it, so I respect his wishes."

Nancy couldn't help remembering the old fairy-tale about Bluebeard, who forbade his beautiful young wife ever to open a certain room in his castle. When she did and discovered its sinister secret— the heads of former wives he had murdered—she almost became another of his victims. Seeing her friend's unhappy face, however, Nancy kept her thoughts to herself.

When the girls returned to the great hall of the castle, Lisa was ready for "elevenses," the British version of a morning snack. Nancy was eager to see the village, but she couldn't persuade Lisa to accompany her.

"You'll enjoy it more by yourself, Nancy."

"Why do you say that?"

"I've told you most of the villagers will hardly speak to me. I think they're more apt to be friendly to you if they don't see us together."

Nancy set off downhill, preferring to stretch her legs rather than borrow Lisa's bike. Polpenny was little more than a cluster of stone cottages, most of them whitewashed and thatch-roofed, circling the cove. All activity seemed to center on the cobbled high street around the harbor, but even that seemed none too busy. There were only two or three wooden docks. Most of the boats were simply drawn up on the stony shingle which sloped down into the water. Coming to the small town hall, she decided to introduce herself to the local constable. "My name's Nancy Drew."

The young policeman nodded and smiled politely. "Yes, ma'am, I know. I'm Constable Kenyon."

Nancy was surprised but went on diffidently, "Then maybe you also know I'm an amateur detective?"

"Yes, Miss. I've read about some of your cases."

"Would you mind if I asked you some questions?"

"Of course not. Please have a chair."

"Thank you." Nancy sat down. "There's a rock musician, Ian Purcell, who stayed in Polpenny while he was getting over his drug habit."

Constable Kenyon nodded again, somewhat tight-lipped. "Yes, ma'am, I know him."

"Have you any idea how recently he was here?"

"In Polpenny? Couldn't say for sure, ma'am. He just camps out, like some of the tourists do, and he often goes back and forth to London."

Nancy explained what had happened to Ian Purcell and asked, "Could he have been here just before he turned up at his rooming house in London?"

The policeman frowned thoughtfully. "Hard to say, ma'am. All I can tell you is I haven't seen him around this past week."

"What about drugs?" Nancy asked. "Are they

much of a problem locally? Does any dealing go on?"

Kenyon shrugged. "It's the tourists who give us headaches more than the locals. There was a pusher arrested in Penzance the other day. That's the only recent case. Mind you, there are rumors that dealing goes on at the old tin-mine engine house."

"Where is that?"

"West of the headland, out near the edge of the moor. You can see the smokestack from the castle. The mine's closed, you see, so the engine house area is all deserted. I've staked it out once or twice at night but I never caught anyone."

Nancy pondered a bit before asking, "One last question, Constable. This may sound silly, but have you ever heard talk of a local witch cult?"

Just for a moment she thought Kenyon's glance flickered. Then his jaw clamped grimly. "There's always gossip of that sort, I reckon, especially here in Cornwall, but there's no such goings-on in Polpenny that I know of."

Nancy thanked him, rose and walked out thoughtfully into the summer sunshine. She was puzzled by the fact that he had known of her sleuthing. How had he found out? From a castle servant?

She wandered about, gazing in shop windows and exploring the byways. The villagers smiled at her and their lilting accents were pleasant to hear. But everyone seemed to know that she was Lady Penvellyn's American friend, and her attempts at conversation were politely rebuffed.

Nancy felt frustrated and annoyed. What on earth could they have against Lisa, and why should such resentment brush off on her?

Finally she turned back toward the harbor. The breeze carried a refreshing tang of salt air. A young man in a tweed sports jacket was chatting with fishermen as they mended their nets. Seeing Nancy, he broke off and came walking toward her.

"Excuse me. You're Nancy Drew, aren't you?"

"Why, yes." Nancy smiled, pleased that someone had finally spoken to her. "How did you know?"

"It's my business to know, you might say. I'm Alan Trevor, a reporter for the *Western Sun*."

Nancy recognized the name of one of England's larger West Country newspapers, having seen it on railway newsstands. "But surely I'm not that well known on this side of the Atlantic."

"You are now." The reporter, husky and clean-shaven, had a brash, smart-alecky manner that nettled Nancy. "In the States you may be a famous girl detective, but over here you're Lance Warrick's latest bird. Warrick's scheduled a gig in Cornwall, so you've come to be near him, right? Officially, of course, you're hunting drug pushers and a gold statuette."

Nancy was breathless with shock and outrage. "I b-b-beg your pardon!" she stuttered angrily.

Trevor grinned. "If it's the bit about Lance

87

Warrick that upsets you, Miss Drew, don't blame me. It's all in the tabloids. All I want to know is whether you've dug up any mystery at the castle?"

"Why not read your trashy tabloids and find out!" Nancy retorted, then turned and walked away.

Angry as she was, Nancy simply had to find out if there was any truth in Alan Trevor's remarks, so she bought a couple of London papers at a village sweet shop. It took only a moment of leafing through the pages to confirm her fears.

Simmering, she trudged back up the road to Penvellyn Castle. Questions were rising in her mind, none of them pleasant to dwell on. Partly to distract herself, Nancy decided to look for the letter that Ethel Bosinny had lost the night before.

From her and the butler's remarks, Nancy knew the bicycle had overturned near a huge old oak tree and clump of shrubbery just to the right of the path leading up to the castle gateway.

To her surprise, she quickly sighted a lavender envelope. It bore the Crowned Heads monogram and was addressed to her at Penvellyn Castle in Lance's handwriting.

Nancy was eager to read the letter in private. Luckily she managed to get up to her room without encountering Lisa or Hugh. To her annoyance, her hands trembled as she opened the envelope.

But there was no letter inside!

Nancy could feel something else, however, small

and hard. She shook it out into the palm of her hand—and caught her breath.

It was a tiny, glassy stone arrowhead . . . *another elf-bolt!*

Surely Lance hadn't sent her this! But if not, who had? Some other member of his group?

Another explanation was possible, Nancy realized. The spook might have filched the envelope after Ethel Bosinny was helped indoors, then removed the letter and inserted the elf-bolt before putting the envelope back during the night.

But why? As a warning to this young American busybody to leave Polpenny Castle and not pry into matters of witchcraft that didn't concern her?

Despite her normal commonsensical outlook, Nancy couldn't shake off a chill of fear that trickled down her spine. Slumping in her chair, she let the elf-bolt and envelope fall into her lap and clasped her hands to keep them from trembling.

What I need, Nancy told herself sternly, is to get so mad that I won't have room to be frightened!

Which was easy enough once she opened those London tabloids and read the leering accounts of her friendship with Lance. One paper ran a photo of them in his sports car escaping the fans outside her hotel. The implication was clear . . . that the American sleuth was the latest addition to Lance Warrick's harem of groupies!

Nancy was furious. What if those reports were to

filter back to America and be read by her dad and Hannah and all her friends in River Heights?

Nancy felt a need to work off her churning emotional energy. Yet she didn't want to be seen by the servants or risk facing Lisa or Hugh in her upset state. To calm herself, she began walking down the corridor, her thoughts in turmoil. No wonder Constable Kenyon knew all about her! Those hateful news stories might even partly explain the villagers' coolness toward her!

She slowed her steps as angry voices drifted toward her. Nancy realized that she was near the Penvellyns' private suite.

"I've told you before—what's in that room is none of your business!" Hugh was saying stormily.

"But why not, if I'm your wife?" Lisa pleaded.

"Because I say so, and I'm your husband! What kind of a marriage do we have if you can't trust me that far?"

"Doesn't trust work both ways? Oh, Hugh, I felt so foolish and ashamed, having to admit to Nancy that you wouldn't even tell *me* why you keep that room shut up and locked!"

"Nancy's here as our guest, not as a detective!" Lord Penvellyn retorted. "Why I choose to keep that room closed is none of her business, either!"

"I'm not a child! You've no right to treat me like one!" Lisa's voice rose and quavered; she sounded on the verge of tears. "What can possibly be in there that's so terrible you can't even confide in me, your wife?!"

"Just take my word, that's all! That room must remain locked to protect my family name and our happiness, do you understand?!" Hugh's hot-tempered words turned cold and grim as he ended, "I want you and your friend to stay away from that room, is that clear?! From now on, I don't even want to hear it mentioned!"

12

Danger in the Dark

Nancy's cheeks burned with embarrassment. It was
bad enough to feel like a snoop whose prying had
caused trouble between a couple she was so fond of.
But to learn of this by eavesdropping, even uninten-
tionally, seemed to make it all the worse!

The teenager turned and fled down the corridor,
fearful that the Penvellyns' door might open at any
moment.

Back in her own room, Nancy brooded over the
mystery. Was the dispute she had just overheard
bitter enough and important enough to have caused
Lisa's unhappiness and loss of health? Surely her
friend's trouble went deeper than mere resentment
over her husband's secrecy, but if so, what was the
real cause?

Neither Lisa nor Hugh appeared at lunch, so

Nancy was left to pick at her salad and cutlet alone. She had just finished her tea and risen from the table when the butler announced Ethel Bosinny.

"I have explained that her ladyship is not feeling well and that Lord Penvellyn is busy in the library working on his book," Landreth told Nancy. "Do you wish to see her, Miss?"

"Yes, of course. Please show her in."

Miss Bosinny's manner by daylight was bluff and hearty. Nancy could well imagine that she might prove slightly overwhelming as a constant companion. "What's wrong with Lisa, my dear?" she demanded. "Another of those deuced headaches?"

"I'm afraid so," Nancy said. "She didn't feel well enough to eat. I imagine she's lying down."

"Then I must go and see her! I know just how to massage her neck and temples to relieve her muscular tensions. And luckily," the elderly woman added, producing a bottle from her shoulder bag, "I've brought along some of my herbal restorative. It always does the poor dear so much good!"

Before Nancy could object or stop her, Ethel Bosinny went striding up the staircase from the great hall and along the upper-floor gallery toward the Penvellyns' private suite.

Lisa was resting on a chaise longue. But she seemed glad to see her visitor and was soon relaxing under the ex-games mistress's skilled touch.

"Would you be kind enough to fetch a glass from

the bathroom, dear," Ethel said to Nancy, "so she can sip some of my herb cordial?"

A thought occurred to the teen sleuth. Could something in the herbal concoction be affecting Lisa's health? Nancy glanced through the medicine cabinet and picked out a small bottle of aspirin. She removed the tablets and rinsed out the bottle, then poured in some of the cordial, capped the bottle again and slipped it into her pocket.

When Nancy returned, Ethel was crooning gently as she massaged Lisa's head. From the latter's contented smile, it appeared that Miss Bosinny's ministrations were having the desired effect. Ethel took the glass of cordial but before she could hold it to her patient's lips, Lisa's head sagged forward and her eyelids closed in slumber.

"Let her sleep, poor lamb," Ethel murmured, "but when she wakes up, be sure she drinks some of this."

After Ethel left, Nancy poured out the concoction.

At dinner, Lisa appeared more cheerful and in better spirits. Hugh, however, was grim-faced and taciturn. Nancy did her best to keep up a flow of conversation, but she was still so depressed over the tabloid news stories that it was hard to maintain a smiling front.

Nancy wrote several letters home that evening, then read a novel until she drifted off to sleep. Her dreams were troubled and she tossed and turned. Suddenly her eyes opened and she sat upright.

A creaking noise echoed from the corridor. What on earth is that? Nancy wondered. Her bedside travel clock showed 1:17 A.M. She threw back the covers, swung her feet to the floor, and pulled on a robe and slippers. Then she peered out of her room down the hall.

At a bend in the corridor, a door stood ajar. Nancy could feel a faint cold draft coming through it. That's the tower door! she reflected. Its creaking hinges indicated it was seldom used. Why would anyone be going up there now?

Curious, Nancy snatched a penlight from her bag and hurried down the hall. Beyond the door, ancient stone steps spiraled upward. She mounted them silently.

Suddenly Nancy stopped short, wide-eyed as she glimpsed a gowned, bare-footed figure above her. *It was Lisa!* Nancy called out to her softly but got no response.

"Lisa—?" she repeated in a louder voice. Her friend continued up the tower stairs. *She's walking in her sleep!* Nancy realized. Her own skin chilled to gooseflesh at the eerie sight.

More curious than ever, and uncertain whether or not to wake her friend, Nancy followed step by step. The climb was exhausting, yet Lisa showed no sign of awakening. She passed a door which, Nancy could see through a window in the tower wall, led out onto a walkway along the battlements. Evidently she was heading for the very top of the tower!

At last she emerged onto the stone roof. Nancy, following her, could see the notched stone parapet surrounding them in the moonlight. Lisa walked straight toward one of the notches.

A gasp of horror rose in Nancy's throat as she suddenly sensed her friend's intention. Nancy choked off the sound before it reached her lips, for fear of waking and startling Lisa into losing her balance. Already Lisa was climbing up into the embrasure or opening in the parapet! Another moment and the sleepwalker would be poised to step off into empty air!

Nancy's heart was thudding in panic. What to do?! There was no time to reason out the wisest course. Acting on blind instinct, she rushed forward and grabbed Lisa around the waist. For a second both girls tottered perilously as Nancy struggled to restrain her friend! Then Lisa seemed to go limp and the two girls sagged backward to safety, collapsing on the stone roof of the tower!

Footsteps were pounding toward them. As the mist of terror cleared from Nancy's eyes, she became aware of a man bending over them. It was Hugh, clad in pajamas and robe, his face still aghast at the heart-stopping drama that had just taken place. "Lisa! Lisa, darling!" he exclaimed in a voice hoarse with emotion. "Thank God you're all right!"

He gathered his young wife tenderly in his arms as if she were a child. Tall and powerfully built as he was, Nancy had wondered earlier if he might be capable of violence when provoked by rage or opposition to his wishes. There was no sign of any such tendency in his nature now. Never had his deep love for Lisa seemed more apparent. He murmured words of gratitude to Nancy. Then, with his wife in his arms, he strode across the roof and started back down the stone steps.

Nancy paused to peer down through the notch in the parapet. The sheer drop to the rocky ground below almost left her giddy! Would Lisa have gone over the brink . . . or would some instinct of self-preservation have awakened her in time? The very thought of what could have happened made Nancy feel sick!

As she turned away, her eyes caught a distant glimmer of light. It was coming from a point somewhere west of the castle. Peering intently, she could make out a tall smokestack in the moonlight. . . . *The engine house of the old abandoned tin mine!* Nancy felt a surge of excitement.

She hurried after Lord Penvellyn and followed him down the tower stairs. In the doorway of the couple's room, she hesitated uncertainly as he deposited his still-sleeping wife on the bed.

"Can I help in any way?"

"I think she'll be all right now, thank you," Hugh replied. "I can't tell you how grateful I am to you,

Nancy, for saving Lisa!" He was clearly unused to making such emotional speeches and spoke in a tone of gruffly awkward sincerity, adding with a shudder, "My God, when I think what might have happened—!"

"Has she ever sleepwalked before?"

"Not that I'm aware of, but . . . who can say?" Hugh shrugged helplessly. "I don't usually wake up at night, but she must have made some slight noise in leaving the room. I awoke, and when I discovered Lisa was gone, I ran out into the hall and saw that the tower door was open."

After talking a while longer, Nancy returned to her own room. But instead of going back to bed, she put on a sweater and jeans. Then, after waiting and listening to make sure no one was up and about, she stole quietly out of the castle.

Lisa's bicycle was leaning against a wall of the courtyard. Nancy mounted it and pedaled off into the darkness. A chilly breeze was blowing in from the sea, making her glad she had worn her sweater. The moon had slipped behind a veil of clouds, but there was light enough to see her way. She took the road that ran near the castle and followed it to the paved highway leading west to Penzance.

When she neared the mine's engine house, Nancy turned off the highway. She parked the bike among some trees and started on foot toward the smokestack, which was visible not far off. Soon the engine house itself came in sight, but she was approaching a blank wall of the old stone building. Nancy circled about till she could see a window. A light still gleamed from within.

Not a sound broke the night's silence, save for the distant beat of surf on the rocky coast.

At last Nancy ventured closer and peered in the window. The light was coming from a lantern, but there was no one inside. The door opened readily. Nancy wrinkled her nose in distaste as she entered. The interior reeked of incense and marihuana!

On the floor lay a broken hypodermic syringe and scattered marihuana butts, indicating recent drug use. But there were other signs that interested her even more. One was a five-sided figure painted on the floor, the "magic pentacle" that witches and wizards stand inside when summoning the occult forces of darkness. On the wall were chalk marks that she recognized as witch symbols.

In this part of Cornwall, it seemed, drug use was closely allied with witchcraft!

Suddenly Nancy froze as she heard a faint, strange melody in the distance. The music had a thin piping quality, like an Irish tin whistle playing an old folk tune. But where could it be coming from, in such a lonely spot this late at night? Nancy felt a chill of fear.

Were the cultists and drug-users who were in the engine house earlier still lurking nearby? And if they were, had they seen her?

She went out again and peered into the darkness.

The moonlight was too dim to see very far, but the piping sound seemed to be coming from the west. She didn't want to use the lantern from the engine house; that would advertise her approach. Better rely on her little purse penlight, Nancy decided.

She started cautiously toward the sound, wondering what she would find. From what she could recall about the landscape she had glimpsed while being driven from the station to the castle, there was nothing out this way but bleak, uninhabited moorland.

Nancy proceeded, step by step, flicking on her penlight now and then to avoid obstacles. The piping sound was moving too, she sensed, drawing her onward. A pang of mistrust shot through her. Suddenly her feet squelched into sticky muck. She tried to back out—only to sink still deeper!

Nancy floundered wildly, but the effort only sank her ankle-deep into the muck. With a gasp of terror she realized, *I've walked into a quicksand bog!*

13

A Whispered Warning

"Help! Help!" Nancy screamed, giving way to blind fear. She knew that her cries might bring the very people she had come to spy on, maybe even the spooky cultist who had sent her the elf-bolt, but any risk seemed preferable to the horror of her present predicament!

Again and again she called out, with no response. As she paused for breath, Nancy became aware that the piping music had stopped. Too late she realized that its only purpose must have been to lure her into the deadly, quaking bog!

For several moments Nancy hovered on the verge of utter panic. Shrill screams rent the air and, with a convulsive shudder, she realized that the screams were coming from her own throat!

If she were to survive, she had to keep her head.

With a steely effort of will, Nancy took a firm grip on her nerves and began to assess her position. By now, her floundering had sunk her at least a foot into the muck. Unless she calmed down, she would soon be up to her knees in the slimy morass!

I must stay still, she decided. It seemed unlikely that anyone other than her unknown enemies would be wandering on the moor at this hour. But sound travels farther at night in open terrain, she had always heard, so there was at least a faint chance that her cries might be heard by a distant passing motorist on the highway.

Nancy took a deep breath, then yelled as loudly as she could. She was hideously aware that with every passing moment she was sinking deeper and deeper into the bog. Her skin crawled as she pictured herself waist-deep in the bog . . . then shoulder-deep and neck-deep, until finally . . . !

Shuddering, Nancy thrust such thoughts from her mind. Somewhere she recalled reading that by lying flat, a victim trapped in quicksand could spread his weight and thus survive much longer. But it seemed a desperate move and she was reluctant to put it to the test, save as a last resort. She decided to continue trying to attract attention. Again she screamed for help as loudly as she could . . . and again.

Suddenly Nancy's heart gave a leap. Was that a sound she had just heard? . . . Yes! Someone was calling back to her! . . . A man's voice!

"This way! Over here!" Nancy cried frantically.

Her eyes caught a distant gleam of light. The glow seemed to widen and grow brighter, and presently she realized that someone was shining a flashlight on her.

The beam shifted away to take the glare out of her eyes, and Nancy was at last able to make out the man who was holding the electric torch. There was something familiar about his voice, but it was only minutes later, after his strong hands had reached out to pull her slowly but surely out of the squelching muck, that she finally recognized who he was. *Alan Trevor, the reporter!*

Nancy sank, gasping and trembling, into his arms, babbling her thanks.

"H-h-how did you happen to hear me?" she quavered.

"I was snooping around the old engine house, checking out some rumors and trying to dig up a story on drug-dealing in Polpenny." Trevor waited in turn for Nancy's explanation of the ghastly plight from which he had just rescued her.

"Y-you've saved my life," she acknowledged shakily, "and I'm more grateful than I can say . . . but could I ask one more favor?"

"Why not?"

"When you write your story about what you saw back there in the engine house, could you leave me out of it . . . at least for now?"

There was a brief silence. Nancy expected him to

bargain for information in exchange. Instead, he merely said, "Okay. The important thing right now is to get you back to the castle."

The reporter not only accompanied her to the spot where she had left Lisa's bicycle, but insisted on following her on foot all the way back to the castle courtyard. Then with a quiet "Good night," he vanished into the moonlit darkness. Nancy was surprised and touched by his behavior.

Luckily, no one was awake in the castle, and Nancy was able to get up to her room without being seen. She showered and sank gratefully into bed, leaving until morning the task of brushing all traces of her night's adventure from her jeans and shoes.

Next day, on the pretext of feeling a bit unwell, Nancy went to visit the local medic. Lisa offered to drive her to his office, but Nancy declined, saying, "I'm hoping that a stroll in the sunshine and fresh air will make me feel better. Just give me directions and let me ramble."

The physician, Dr. Carradine, occupied an old stone house on the outskirts of Polpenny. He turned out to be a tall, sandy-haired man with tired eyes that suggested a busy practice.

"Lady Penvellyn called to tell me you were coming, Miss Drew," he said when Nancy was seated in his surgery. "What seems to be the trouble?"

"Nothing with me, thank goodness. It's Lisa

herself I'm worried about. Would it be all right to consult you about her health?"

"Hmm . . . normally the answer to that question would be no. But I realize you two are old friends, and she has mentioned to me that her mother's very concerned." Carradine frowned and steepled his fingers. "Frankly, Lisa's not well. She's very run down. I've prescribed a course of vitamins and food supplements to build her up physically, but her problem may be emotional."

Nancy nodded thoughtfully. "Yes, that's occurred to her mother too. But is there any chance she could be *taking* something harmful to her health?"

Carradine's frown deepened. "You mean drugs?"

"No, something that Lisa doesn't even suspect may be harmful." Nancy took out the aspirin bottle that she had filled with Ethel Bosinny's elixir. "This is an herb tonic she's been taking. It's probably perfectly wholesome, but, well, perhaps there's something in it that disagrees with her, or that she may be allergic to."

The doctor uncapped the bottle and sniffed its contents. "Hard to say offhand. I've never tested Lisa for allergies. But suppose I have this analyzed and let you know the results."

Nancy thanked him, not mentioning that she had removed the bottle from Lisa's room and poured out the undrunk glassful after Ethel Bosinny left. "One more question, Dr. Carradine. Lisa walked in her sleep last night. What would cause that?"

"I'm no psychiatrist, Miss Drew, but it sounds like an emotional problem she can't cope with, something that festers in her subconscious and disturbs her rest. Let me know if it continues."

As she trudged back to the castle, her thoughts distracted her from enjoying the bright morning and the beautiful scenery of the little Cornish fishing village. As sometimes happened when investigating a mystery, Nancy had the feeling that an important link in the evidence was staring her in the face . . . but what was it?

Even more depressing were the lurid news stories about her and Lance Warrick. Nancy had tried to shut them out of her mind, but they were becoming too blatant to ignore. Hopefully, and against her better judgment, she had picked up a couple of papers at a village newsstand to see if the topic might have faded from public view as quickly as it arose. Instead, she saw the rumor mills were busier than ever!

Back at Penvellyn Castle that afternoon, as she huddled in an overstuffed chair in the sitting room, Nancy realized miserably that the story was now being played up in newspapers all over Britain. She had already heard herself described on the television news as "Lance Warrick's newest girlfriend—a Yank female private eye who combines curves with brains!"

Most painful of all was an article in a rock magazine that a castle maid brought back from the nearby resort town of St. Ives. It claimed to tell the "inside story" of Lance's latest sizzling romance and informed its avid readers that the American girl detective, Nancy Drew, had fallen head over heels in love with the rock king in New York and had pursued him across the Atlantic, hoping to wangle a proposal of marriage!

Almost as bad in Nancy's eyes was the way her stay at Penvellyn Castle was played up and sensationalized. The Golden Mab was dragged in, to hype her detective role. One tabloid even hinted that Lord and Lady Penvellyn might be mixed up in a high-society criminal ring suspected of dealing in stolen art objects!

Another news story, even more startling to Nancy, suggested that she had come to the castle to investigate sordid rumors of a satanic witch cult!

Several press photographers had already made vain trips to the castle. As the day wore on, the phone rang incessantly until Hugh ordered it left off the hook.

There was little doubt in Nancy's mind who was responsible for the flood of publicity. Hadn't Lance himself said that Jane Royce was the best press agent in the business? *Got a sixth sense for what'll make the headlines, that girl—she knows how to squeeze every drop of press coverage out of any angle that comes along!*

Nancy had to squeeze her eyes shut tight to keep

from crying whenever she thought of that night on the town with Lance and the tender way their lips had melted together. Obviously he'd been using her from the very first!

"Nancy dear, you mustn't let this business about Lance Warrick upset you so," Lisa crooned. "It'll blow over as quickly as it started."

Nancy squeezed her friend's hand gratefully. At least it was a step in the right direction, she reflected, for Lisa to forget her own troubles.

At one point, Lisa even suggested calling in Ethel Bosinny to give Nancy a soothing massage. "It's really relaxing, Nancy. Ethel learned physical therapy while she was teaching sports."

Nancy smiled wanly. "I don't think so, Lisa, but thanks."

"All right then, suit yourself," she said with a playful smile to offset her crisp tone, as if chiding a stubborn child. "But I want you in tip-top shape for my dinner party tonight."

"Tonight? Good grief, Lisa, why didn't you warn me! Who's coming?"

"You might say my only friends in Polpenny. Ethel, for one, and Dr. Carradine, plus the local business tycoon, Ivor Roscoe—'Squire' Roscoe, they call him—and his wife, Diane."

Nancy promptly snapped out of her downbeat mood. The upstairs maid helped her do her hair and laid out her chic black party dress.

Ethel Bosinny, who arrived shortly before seven, evidently had also done her best to dress for the occasion. Gone were her tweed suit and stout brogues, replaced by a livid purple gown almost indecently low cut and a jangly copper necklace. She had even applied lipstick.

Next to appear was Dr. Carradine. Nancy found him easy to talk to and learned that he was a widower.

Ivor and Diane Roscoe arrived last. Diane, a quiet brunette, was younger than her husband and attractive enough to have been a movie star. The squire himself was a heavyset man of forty, with a leonine mane and trim pointed beard.

As they chatted at the candlelit dinner table, the talk turned to Cornwall and its traditions of seafaring and mining. "Ivor, by the way, owns the Polpenny tin mine," Hugh remarked to Nancy.

"How interesting!" She told the others what she had learned from Colonel Tremayne.

Squire Roscoe nodded. "It was Cornish tin and copper that brought the Bronze Age to Britain. Not much ore being taken out nowadays, though. We exported many of our best miners to America. My father was the last owner to operate the Polpenny mine full-time. Now it's shut down."

"Which doesn't mean Ivor's retired," Hugh added with a chuckle. "He runs a London ad agency, along with several other businesses."

109

"He's also active in the arts," Ethel beamed approvingly. "You must get him or Diane to show you around their private gallery, dear."

"I'd love that." The guests had politely avoided any reference to the embarrassing news stories about Nancy. But now she boldly decided to bring up one aspect of those stories herself. Ethel had just given her an opening. "I suppose you've seen the Golden Mab at the Tate?" she asked Roscoe. "I'm told she was the Goddess of the Witches."

A jarring silence ensued. It was broken by Diane hastily murmuring, "I, er, imagine everyone in England's seen it by now, with all the press and television coverage it's received."

"Do you think it's possible a mate to it could have turned up here in Cornwall?" Nancy persisted.

Roscoe shrugged curtly. "'Fraid that's beyond my expertise."

"A man named Ian Purcell claims to have seen such a statuette," Nancy went on, "and I understand he stayed here in Polpenny when he was getting over his drug habit. Was he a patient of yours, Doctor?"

Dr. Carradine nodded. "The rock musician? Yes, he came to me for treatment, but I couldn't persuade him to take the full cure. Still, he seemed to be recovering."

When dinner was over, the ladies adjourned to the drawing room while the men lingered for cigars. Nancy was startled when Diane drew her aside.

"I can't explain just now, Miss Drew," she whispered with a nervous glance over her shoulder, "but please be careful! Polpenny's a very ingrown community. You may stir up a great deal of trouble!"

Was this intended as a tactful hint, Nancy wondered . . . or a veiled warning?

Next morning she decided to venture again into the village, despite the flood of publicity. She felt she would be taking the cowardly way out to hide her face at the castle. A stroll would also enable her to pay another visit to Dr. Carradine.

"How nice to see you again, Miss Drew," the medic greeted her in his consulting room.

"I was wondering if you might have had any report yet on that herbal elixir?"

"Yes, the chemist called just a short time ago. He said it seems to be composed of harmless vegetable ingredients, though of course that still leaves the possibility of an allergic reaction."

Nancy walked away thoughtfully from the doctor's house. On the village high street, she stopped short, her heart thumping. A sleek red sports car had just pulled up near the harbor. A lean, sardonically handsome young man with spiky blond hair jumped out and came striding toward her.

It's Lance! Nancy realized in sudden panic.

The rock star flashed a brilliant smile and reached out to embrace her. "Nancy, luv!"

His arms dropped as he saw how she froze.

"Darling, what's wrong?"

111

"Do you need to ask after all that sleazy publicity your talented press agent stirred up?"

Lance looked genuinely astonished. "What difference does that make? Have you any idea how many birds would give their eye teeth to bask in the limelight as Lance Warrick's newest sweetheart?!"

"Not this bird!" Nancy retorted, stung that he should dare to offer such justification.

She turned to walk away. Lance started after her, reaching out for her arm. "Look, my sweet, I took this gig in Cornwall even though the rest of the group wasn't too keen on the idea just to be near you! Can you blame me if the press draws the obvious conclusions?!"

Nancy shook off his hand scornfully. "Am I supposed to believe Jane Royce dreamed all this up without your full approval? Please understand once and for all, Lance—I am *not* one of your groupies! "

14

Night Sight

This time the rock king did not follow her as she hurried off down the high street. Nancy's cheeks were flaming. She felt as if the whole village of Polpenny must have overheard their quarrel. *Why on earth did I have to go and lose my temper?!* she asked herself regretfully.

In her wretched, almost tearful mood, Nancy was momentarily tongue-tied when Alan Trevor stepped out into her path. "Come with me, Miss Drew," he said softly. "There's a tearoom just round the corner. I promise not to ask any questions."

Almost numbly Nancy let herself be led away.

"That was very kind of you, Mr. Trevor," she said once they were seated and she had regained her composure. "Now I'm doubly in your debt. I'm sorry I was so short with you the other day."

"Don't be silly, I'm the one who should apologize. I've probably seen too many loudmouthed reporters in films. I'm not like that at all—really, cross my heart."

Nancy was able to smile. "What are you like?"

"Just a typical thick-headed Cornishman." They both laughed. "Which reminds me, if I could tempt you into having lunch, they do a very nice line in Cornish pasties here."

Nancy discovered that these were delicious dollops of meat and potatoes baked in dough, which Cornish housewives used to pack in their miner-husbands' lunch pails. As she sampled one, Nancy also discovered that she was hungry.

"Be honest, Mr. Trevor—" she said presently.

"Alan, please," he interrupted.

"All right. Alan. You must have spent some time asking questions around Polpenny, trying to dig up material for a story about me."

He looked sheepish. "That's how I earn my living, Miss Drew."

"Nancy, please. I only wanted to ask if you have any idea why the villagers won't speak to Lady Penvellyn?"

The reporter looked startled, then thoughtful. "Is that a fact? I didn't realize it."

"Are you enough of a native for them to trust you and tell you why?"

Alan Trevor chuckled. "Hard to say in Cornwall. I was born and raised in Mousehole, where they say the last Cornish-speaker was born, which is not exactly the same as being a native of Polpenny. But I'll see what I can find out."

Nancy decided to press her luck. "While you're at it, perhaps you'd be kind enough to check out a crazy story that ran in a tabloid called *The U.K. Flash.* It hinted at a local witch cult. Could you find out who wrote that, and why?"

Trevor's eyes glinted with interest. She knew he was mentally connecting her question with what had happened at the engine house. "To quote a Yank phrase, you've got it, Nancy!"

When she returned to Penvellyn Castle, Nancy saw a sightseeing bus parked in the courtyard. A uniformed guide was herding a group of tourists into the castle. On the spur of the moment she joined them.

The tour guide's memorized spiel contained enough facts to hold her interest, but Nancy had something else in mind. As he droned on, she found an opportunity to slip away from the group.

Scurrying down a branching corridor, she headed for the locked room. As part of her detective skills, Nancy had learned a good deal about locksmithing, and in an emergency, she could pick the average lock.

The one on the stout, iron-bound oak door, however, resisted all her efforts. It was obviously too massive and unique in design to yield to an ordinary picklock. But as she was about to replace

115

the lockpicking device in her handbag, something about it caught Nancy's eye.

The pick was glistening with fresh oil!

"Well, well, well!" she muttered. "Somebody must have gone in here recently!"

As she walked into the great hall of the castle, Landreth the butler hailed her. "Ah, Miss Drew, you've arrived just in time! A gentleman wishes to speak to you on the phone."

"Did he say who he is?"

"A Mr. Lance Warrick, ma'am. This is the third time he's called."

Nancy's chin shot up and her sapphire eyes turned icy. "Please ask him not to call again."

"Very good, Miss Drew."

Lisa had overheard them. She caught up with Nancy on the stairs. "Don't be upset, Nan," she begged, slipping an arm around the teenager's waist.

"I'm not. I just saw him in the village, Lisa, and . . . it was rather unpleasant. My own fault probably."

"Never mind. Ethel Bosinny's coming over this evening. She's promised to give us a séance."

"A *séance!*" Nancy looked at her friend in surprise. "You mean she's a—a psychic medium?"

"Good question. All I can say is, she goes into trances, and she's told both Hugh and me some rather odd things. Anyhow, it should be fun."

Nancy was skeptical. Nevertheless, she joined in the experiment, and the Penvellyns and their two guests joined hands around a small table in the drawing room after dinner.

All lights had been extinguished, except for twin candles glowing on the mantel. Miss Bosinny had brought a special mood record to play on the castle's old-fashioned phonograph. It featured a soprano vocalist singing in a sweet, reedy voice to the music of a Welsh harp. Nancy found the overall effect distinctly eerie.

Presently a faint moan came from Ethel Bosinny's lips. This was followed by a woman's voice quite unlike her own hoarse, hearty tones:

"Nay, I am not a witch! . . . You lie, ye black-hearted rogue! . . . Torture me if ye like, but I'll never confess to such foul lies!"

Nancy felt the skin of her arms prickling into gooseflesh. Her eyes met Lisa's. Even in the semi-darkness, she noticed that her friend was looking pale and uneasy. Both girls gave a nervous start as the voice issuing from Ethel's throat suddenly broke into a shrill, long-drawn-out scream!

Hugh leaped to his feet. The music had ceased playing, and the needle was clicking soundlessly in the groove. He lifted the phonograph arm and switched on the lights.

Ethel Bosinny had opened her eyes. Lisa and Nancy were holding her hands and stroking her.

"What happened, Ethel?" Hugh inquired gently.

"I—I'm not sure," she croaked in a hoarse, terrified voice. "I had the most *ghastly* vision!"

"Of what?"

"I saw a black horned devil figure! It was shooting arrows of fire—at me and—and *Nancy!*"

Lisa gasped. Nancy's throat had gone dry, as she thought of the elf-bolt she had found in the lavender envelope.

Nancy lay awake that night, unable to sleep. At last she got out of bed and tiptoed toward the window. The faint sound of a boat engine had just reached her ears through the night air. She pressed her face to the pane, peering out into the moonlit darkness.

To her amazement, a boat was gliding in toward the foot of the headland on which the castle stood! Presently it passed out of view, too far below to be glimpsed beneath the steep rocky slope.

Nancy waited for ten long minutes, but the craft failed to reappear. She was about to withdraw from the window when she saw something else that made her freeze in amazement.

A slender gowned figure with flowing blond hair was walking slowly out toward the point of the headland.

"It's Lisa!" Nancy gasped, half aloud. "She's sleepwalking again!"

15

Undine

The sudden realization of her friend's danger convulsed Nancy into action. In frantic haste, she pulled on her jeans, sweater and moccasins, then ran out into the corridor, screaming for Hugh.

He appeared in the doorway before she reached their suite. "Lisa's heading for the cliffs!" Nancy cried.

Seconds later they were running out of the courtyard. Lisa's wraithlike figure was visible in the distance. Hugh lengthened his stride, his long legs pumping like pistons, and soon left Nancy far behind. Her heart gave a lurch of fear. Lisa would soon reach the brink of the cliff!

Nancy breathed a silent prayer. As if in answer, her friend paused, then raised a hand to her forehead in a gesture of perplexity. Within seconds

119

Hugh had caught up with her and enfolded her tightly in his arms.

"Wh-where am I? . . . What are we doing out here?" Lisa was muttering as Nancy joined them.

"We decided to take a midnight stroll, don't you remember?" Hugh joked tenderly. In her dazed state Lisa seemed to accept this far-fetched explanation.

Nancy was thoughtful as they returned to the castle. Was it possible that Lisa had faked both her sleepwalking episodes to arouse her husband's sympathy? The idea seemed hateful to Nancy, and none too plausible. Surely her friend was not that skillful an actress to stage such terrifying and utterly convincing scenes!

During the night, another idea came to Nancy's mind. It had to do with the "connecting link" idea she had been groping for. Rising early, Nancy went to the castle library and looked up *Hypnosis* and *Suggestion* in the encyclopedia.

Afterward she used the telephone. Alan Trevor had told her he roomed in Penzance. Nancy called the nearest office of the *Western Sun*, which turned out to be in Plymouth, and learned his phone number. Then she called him.

"Nancy! What a pleasant surprise!" the reporter crowed. "Good thing you called—I have some information for you."

"I have something to tell you too, Alan."

"Good! Then meet me at the tearoom in Polpenny at 10:30 sharp and we'll swap news!"

Nancy was impatient for the meeting. As they ate breakfast, the reporter began, "You asked me to check out that witch bit in *The U.K. Flash*. Well, it was written by a bloke named Coburn, an old Fleet Street hand. My boss knows him, so he called and asked where he got the yarn."

"What did he find out?"

"Coburn claimed there actually *were* such rumors floating around a couple of years ago."

"About Penvellyn Castle?"

"Not exactly. They involved the old Lord Penvellyn, Hugh Penvellyn's uncle. Apparently he was rather an old troublemaker. Rumors were circulating among his London pals that he was into witchcraft and devil worship. Coburn admitted to my editor that he was just trying to rework that old gossip."

"I see." Nancy pondered a moment. "That's very interesting, Alan. Thanks."

"There's more to come. My boss suggested I check out the local history angle to see if there's any tradition of witchcraft in Polpenny, so I went to the library in Penzance."

"And is there?"

"Is there ever! Back in the early 1700's during the witch trials, the mistress of Penvellyn Castle was a Lady Phoebe Penvellyn. Somehow she got herself accused by the official witch-hunters."

121

Nancy's eyes widened. "What happened?"

"They tortured her into confessing that she was the leader of a witch coven here in Polpenny. And before she died, she incriminated several villagers —who were later burned at the stake."

"How horrible!" Nancy shuddered. She was hearing again the strange unearthly voice that had come from Ethel Bosinny's lips during her trance.

"I'm not sure whether all that helps you any." Alan studied her face. "I mean, you *are* trying to unravel some sort of mystery, aren't you?"

Nancy nodded. "Yes, and if I succeed, I'll tell you as much as I'm allowed to, Alan." Then she described what she had seen from the castle window during the night without mentioning Lisa's sleepwalking. "Are you any good at boating?" she added.

The reporter chuckled. "My dear girl! My old dad skippered a fishing trawler—and you ask me that? Don't you know that Drake, Hawkins and all the great English seadogs were West Countrymen!"

"Then let's rent a boat and see if we can find out what that boat I glimpsed last night was up to."

"On one condition."

"Name it."

"That you'll come out with me this evening."

"Agreed, Mr. Trevor!"

Within half an hour they were sailing windward out of the harbor in a small dinghy. Alan, at the tiller, steered them skillfully between the two stone breakwaters. Later, as they neared the jutting

122

headland, he lowered the sail and unshipped the oars to row them closer inshore.

"Can you remember the boat's exact course?"

Nancy shaded her eyes and gazed up at Castle Penvellyn to locate her bedroom window. Then she pointed precisely. "It was in *that* direction!"

Even with the sea so blue and relatively calm, the gentle waves flung up foam and spray as they splashed against the jagged rocks. Alan approached the rocks with great caution. "They're like deadly fangs," he remarked. "They can devour a boat like matchwood, or even a large ship, if the wind's up enough!"

"Look, Alan!" Nancy cried. "See that shelving outcrop about ten feet above the water?"

"What about it?"

"Do you see an opening just below it?"

The reporter squinted intently. The dazzling sunshine and the shadow of the outcrop made it difficult to discern the details of the rock formation, but his face suddenly reflected her own excitement. "You're right! There *is* an opening!"

He maneuvered as close to the rocks as he dared, then dropped a hemp fender-guard over the side and anchored the boat in place by wrapping some rope around a granite spur that stuck out above the water.

"Think you can make it from here?" Alan inquired.

"I'll try if you will!"

While he held their craft steady with a boathook, Nancy scrambled nimbly ashore over the rocks slippery with seaweed. Alan followed.

Though wet from flying spray, both were exhilarated. Having made it safely this far, the rest of the way seemed easy by comparison. The jagged cliff face offered ample footing as they clawed their way toward the opening.

Alan entered first, then reached out a hand for Nancy. She switched on her penlight, which she had brought from her shoulder bag, and shone it around.

They gasped at the sight it revealed. They were in a dank cavern littered with pieces of nautical gear: several large empty casks, coils of rope, a pair of rotting oars, moldy canvas, a rusty cutlass and equally rusty tools that might have belonged to an old-time ship's carpenter, and a brassbound sea chest stenciled with the name *Undine*.

"Must be the ship it came off," said Alan.

"But how did it get up here?"

"Wreckers' work, I imagine."

Nancy threw him a puzzled glance. "Say that again?"

"Haven't you ever heard of the old Cornish wreckers?" When she shook her head, he went on. "They were land pirates, back in the days of sailing ships. In bad weather they'd light fake beacon fires to lure ships close inshore. Then when the vessels piled up on the rocks, they'd loot the wreckage."

Nancy shivered. "Sounds inhuman!"

"Those were cruel times. Back then, wrecking and smuggling were major Cornish industries."

"What about *that*?" Nancy aimed her flashlight at a strange marking on the grotto wall. It looked like the head of a pig.

Alan stared at it, half amused, half puzzled. "Beats me. . . . Maybe that represented the contemporary image of His Majesty's Coast Guards."

Nancy chuckled but could not help feeling that the odd drawing might be significant. The cavern appeared not to extend very deeply into the cliffside, and they could find no further clue to whatever last night's visitor—or visitors—might have been after.

Nevertheless, Nancy's thoughts were busy as they sailed back into the harbor. Alan's mention of smuggling had given her a possible new lead to the mystery. Before returning to the castle, she stopped in to see Constable Kenyon again.

"Could you tell me if Ian Purcell was ever in trouble with the law over drugs?" she inquired.

"Not here he wasn't. I'd have to check with Central Records at Scotland Yard to know for sure."

"If you would, I'd appreciate it," said Nancy.

Constable Kenyon was too young not to respond to a pretty face. Besides, this American girl, by all accounts, had quite a record at cracking difficult criminal cases. She might be onto something big. "I'll see what I can find out, Miss Drew," he promised.

When she arrived back at Penvellyn Castle, Nancy made a phone call to Huntley & Dawlish, the law firm her father had mentioned with offices at Lincoln's Inn, one of London's famous Inns of Court.

Mr. Dawlish answered promptly. "It's a pleasure to hear from the daughter of such a distinguished American colleague. How can I help you, Miss Drew?"

Nancy described what she and Alan had seen in the cliffside cavern. "Am I right in thinking that Lloyd's of London keeps a record of all British shipwrecks?"

"They do, indeed. At any rate, of ships that they themselves have insured."

"Could you possibly find out if they've any record of an old-time sailing ship called *Undine?*"

"I've friends at Lloyd's," said the barrister. "If they do, I'm sure there'll be no difficulty in digging up a full report."

Nancy thanked him and hung up.

Lisa was intrigued to hear about Nancy's date that evening. Late that afternoon as Nancy was preparing for a refreshing bath, she was called to the phone. It was Constable Kenyon.

"I've just learned from Scotland Yard, Miss, that Ian Purcell does have a record. He was arrested last year for drug-pushing, but was released for lack of evidence."

Nancy was thoughtful as she bathed and dressed. When Alan Trevor called to pick her up, he gazed at her in obvious admiration.

She smiled at him as she got into the car. "Where are we going?"

Her heart skipped a beat as he replied, "To watch the Crowned Heads perform at Porthcurno."

16

The Grotto Symbol

Nancy stared distractedly at her escort. "What's this all about, Alan? Are you just after another news story? Is that why you asked me out?"

He reached out impulsively for her hand. "No! Believe me, Nancy! I do have a reason for taking you to the concert, but I—I'd rather not say why just yet. Will you trust me?"

Nancy swallowed hard. "All right, if that's what you want. . . . After all, we did make a bargain."

"Good!" Shifting into gear, he drove out of the courtyard.

In addition to all its other features, Cornwall was also a land of flowers, Nancy had noticed. Their scent filled the soft night air. But as she and Alan rode through the darkness, her thoughts were in a turmoil. She suddenly realized that she had come to like this friendly young Brit reporter very much . . . but was he, too, using her for his own selfish ends, just as Lance Warrick had?

She bit her lip as the rock star's face rose in her mind. The thought of him made her blood race, throwing her emotions into even greater confusion.

Whom did she *really* want to be with tonight? Alan Trevor? . . . or Lance? Miserably, Nancy found she couldn't answer her own question.

The Minack Theater, where the concert was to take place, caught Nancy by surprise. It was an open-air amphitheater carved from a rocky cliff that sloped down to Porthcurno Bay, not far from Land's End, the westernmost tip of England. Under the stars, with the murmuring, dark purple sea for a backdrop, if offered a breathtaking spectacle.

Eager rock fans were already overflowing the theater's capacity and lining the clifftops. Alan led Nancy down a secluded path to the narrow beach, which was less crowded, and managed to rent folding chairs near the performers' dressing room.

A roar of applause went up as the Crowned Heads emerged in costume into the brilliantly lit stage area. But Lance suddenly stopped short. He had just caught sight of Nancy with Alan Trevor.

Nancy sensed that he was already keyed up for the night's show, and seeing her with a rival had evidently triggered a flare of emotion. Lance strode toward them, his jaw jutting angrily.

"What the devil are you doing with my bird?!"

129

Alan rose swiftly to face him. "Cool it, mate!"

Stagehands and the rest of the group moved between them fast before a fight could erupt.

"Sorry about that," Alan whispered to Nancy as he took his seat again. "Want to leave?"

Fortunately all spotlights were on the stage now, leaving them in darkness which hid her confusion and embarrassment. "No, of course not."

Alan squeezed her hand. "Good girl!"

The Crowned Heads' performance was every bit as exciting here as it had been in New York. Lance, if anything, seemed to project himself across the footlights with even more violent intensity.

But later, as she and Alan drove back to Polpenny, Nancy found she could remember very little of the show. The pounding beat of the music, the colorful costumes and psychedelic lights—above all, her own turbulent emotions—had left her with only a blur of wild images.

When he stopped his car in the castle courtyard, Alan slipped an arm around Nancy's shoulders. "You're still wondering why I took you to the concert tonight?"

"Yes, I am."

"I reckon I wanted to see with my own eyes how you feel about Lance Warrick."

"And what did you learn?"

The young reporter shrugged helplessly. "I still don't know. All I know is that I—I'm mad about you, Nancy!"

He drew her close and kissed her. Nancy resisted at first, then found herself yielding willingly to his embrace.

When they said good night moments later, she was less sure than ever which of the two she found more attractive, Lance or Alan.

Next morning, partly to divert her unruly thoughts, Nancy went to visit the Roscoes. Lisa had given her directions, and their beautiful Tudor-style manor house, within sight of the village, was impossible to miss.

Ivor Roscoe, whose business schedule seemed not all that demanding, was at home, and so was his wife Diane. They received her in their sunlit sitting room over tea and biscuits.

"Well, and how is your detective work progressing?" Nancy thought she caught a sarcastic undertone to her bearded host's remark.

"In a way that's why I'm here," she replied. "To ask you a question about the tin mine."

"My dear Miss Drew, fire away!"

"The underground workings were quite extensive, I suppose?"

He frowned, obviously intrigued by her question. "Indeed they were! But why do you ask?"

"Is it possible one of the tunnels might have extended as far as the castle headland?"

Ivor Roscoe looked startled. "No . . . no, I hardly think so. I'd have to check the company blue-

131

prints to be sure, but most of the workings ran northward under the moor."

Nancy had hoped to find Mrs. Roscoe alone and in a mood to explain her cryptic remark the night of the dinner party. Since there was no chance of that, she soon made an excuse to leave.

Ambling through the steep, cobbled streets of the village, Nancy pondered the puzzle of the seacliff grotto. Why had the nocturnal boatman gone there? A connecting tunnel to the mine might have provided an answer, but now it seemed the—

"Nancy, luv!"

The titian-haired teen came out of her pensive trance to find herself face to face with Alan Trevor. "Alan!" she gasped, then burst out laughing. "I was so wrapped up in my thoughts I never even saw you coming."

"So I gathered from that frown on your face."

Together they strolled toward Polpenny Harbor.

"Alan," Nancy said, "does much smuggling still go on around here nowadays?"

The reporter shrugged. "Some. Dope from the Caribbean, for example, and there's always the odd case of French wine or brandy being sneaked in across the Channel."

"*Brandy!*" Nancy stopped abruptly as a wild thought flashed through her mind. "Alan, are you game to take me out to that sea cavern again?"

"Love to. Just say when."

"I'll have to go back first and change into something more practical. Make it after lunch—say, 2:00!"

At the castle, Nancy had just finished chatting with Hugh and Lisa and was about to rise from the lunch table, when the butler summoned her to the phone. The London barrister, Mr. Dawlish, was calling to report what he had learned about a sailing ship called *Undine*.

"My friend at Lloyd's says the brig *Undine* sailed from Boston in 1702, bound for Bristol. But it stopped at Cork, Ireland, to pick up an archeological treasure—"

"What sort of treasure?" Nancy put in tensely.

"A recently unearthed figurine. It was being sent to Cambridge University for study. Unfortunately *Undine* never reached Bristol. She was believed to have foundered in a storm, somewhere off the western coast of England."

"Then both crew and cargo were lost?" Despite her excitement, Nancy tried to keep her voice even.

"Yes, but a passenger survived—a young American girl named Phoebe Harwood."

Phoebe! . . . Phoebe *Harwood!* Nancy's heart was thumping. "That's a tremendous help, Mr. Dawlish! Thank you ever so much!"

Nancy could hardly wait to get back to the cavern. Alan was waiting on the dock, and their dinghy was soon gliding seaward. They moored the boat to the rocks as before, then clambered into the cliffside grotto. Both had brought flashlights.

"Are you going to tell me now about this sudden brilliant inspiration you had?" said Alan.

Nancy shone her beam at the snouty pig face on the wall. "Liquids like brandy or rum used to be shipped in large casks, right?"

He nodded. "So?"

"Do you know what those casks were called?"

"Sure, Hogsh—" Alan broke off as his jaw dropped open. *"Hogsheads!"*

"Correct. So let's check on those hogsheads right over there."

"We already did when we came here before. They're empty."

"Then let's find out what's underneath them."

The casks were standing on an old tarpaulin. When both were cleared away, a narrow crevice was revealed in the rocky floor of the cave. It appeared to slope downward at an angle.

"I'll go first," said Alan. He tied some of the ancient rope around his waist and Nancy let it out as he squirmed down through the hole.

Presently he shouted back up. "Come on, it's safe! I'll catch you!"

Nancy slid out of the narrow passageway into his arms. When he set her down, she saw that they were standing on the narrow bank of an underground stream which flowed off into darkness.

"Let's explore it, Alan!"

He shook his head. "Not now. Wouldn't be safe.

The tide's starting to come in. We might be trapped without scuba gear."

"When's the next low tide?"

"Tomorrow morning."

Nancy grinned. "Meet you at 9:00 sharp then, on the dock!"

17

Secret Altar

Nancy spent the rest of the afternoon in a fever of impatience. Lisa sensed her overcharged mood.

"You haven't made up with your rock-star boyfriend by any chance?" she probed.

Nancy smiled. "No, and you mustn't draw any conclusions from the fact that I attended the Crowned Heads concert last night, either."

"Then what goes on, Nan? Or shouldn't I pry?"

"It's no secret. I've a date to go scuba diving tomorrow morning with Alan Trevor—and something tells me it could be very exciting!"

Lady Penvellyn stretched luxuriously and stifled a yawn. "The most exciting thing around here will be a tour group that's coming to the castle before noon. I'll have to try and coax Hugh out of working so hard on his book!"

Her friend was looking better, Nancy thought happily. Lisa's color had improved and her long blond hair was brushed to a glossy sheen. Suddenly Nancy slapped her forehead. "What an idiot! If I'm going diving, I'll have to rent some scuba gear before all the shops close. Where would be the best place to go, Lisa?"

"Penzance probably. Take the car."

Scuba diving is a popular sport along the Cornish coast, and Nancy had no difficulty in outfitting herself with equipment. She was loading everything into Hugh's vintage roadster when she looked up to meet the curious gaze of Mrs. Roscoe.

"Why, hello, Diane! Imagine meeting you here!"

"It *is* a surprise, but what a pleasant one! Are you planning some underwater sightseeing?"

"You could call it that, I guess." Nancy had an odd feeling that the other woman might not have spoken at all if she hadn't been caught staring. "Can I offer you a lift back to Polpenny?"

"No, thanks. I have my car."

Before returning to the castle, Nancy stopped off at Polpenny Harbor to stow her scuba gear aboard the rented dinghy.

Lisa greeted her as she arrived back at the castle. "Get everything you need?"

"Yes, I think so. I saw Diane Roscoe, by the way."

"I know. She called just a few minutes ago and told me. She sounded very interested in your scuba expedition tomorrow morning."

137

Shortly before 9:00 the next morning, Nancy bicycled into the village. Alan was nowhere in sight, so she strolled back and forth on the shingle, watching the fishermen at work.

By 9:30 the reporter still had not appeared. Nancy was growing restless. There was a telephone call box nearby on a corner of the high street. She decided to try his number in Penzance. She heard the phone ringing for a long time at the other end of the line without answer.

On the off chance that she might have dialed incorrectly, she tried again. Still no answer. Nancy figured that if Alan wasn't at home, he must have overslept and was probably driving to Polpenny at this very moment, with one foot jammed on the gas.

But half an hour later, Nancy was fuming. Surely Alan hadn't chickened out! Or had he?

Once again she tried Alan's number. She let the ringing go on and on, determined to make him answer.

But at last Nancy reasoned, All right, so Alan isn't coming; no sense throwing a tantrum. She decided to sail out to the cavern and explore the underground stream by herself.

Squaring her shoulders, she started back to the dock, then stopped. A sleek red sports car had just driven up, with a man and a girl in it. The girl was Jane Royce, and the driver, Lance Warrick, was getting out to speak to Nancy. "Nancy!"

She faced him, unable to find her voice.

"I—I just wanted to apologize for . . . for what happened the other night." For once the rock king seemed to have lost his cool self-assurance. "Where are you going?" he added lamely.

"Out in a boat."

"May I come?" Nancy shot a quizzical glance at his honey-haired companion, and he added quickly, "Never mind her! May I come?"

"I'm going scuba diving."

Lance's lean, high-cheekboned face brightened to a smile. "Terrific! That's my favorite sport. I have full kit in the boot of my car. I always come prepared when I'm anywhere near the coast."

Nancy shrugged and tried to sound indifferent. "Suit yourself, then."

He turned back hastily to his car. As she walked away, she heard Jane Royce exclaim angrily to Lance, "Just what do you think you're doing?"

"What's it look like, duckie? I'm going diving."

"And what am *I* supposed to do?"

"You really want a suggestion?"

Nancy stifled a smile. Lance joined her on the dock with his gear. As they shoved off in the dinghy, he began speaking urgently. "I must've been out of my mind to take you for granted, Nancy luv, and to let Jane Royce talk me into that stupid publicity campaign! I reckon I'm so used to that rock scene groupie mentality, I can't even recognize a nice girl when I meet one!"

139

He took Nancy's shoulder to make her turn and face him. "I found out, darling, just how much you do mean to me! Will you take me back," he pleaded, "and let me try to make things between us the way they were before?"

"Maybe," Nancy said, her own eyes twinkling. "But you'd better watch the tiller and haul in the main sheet, or you'll run us right into the breakwater!"

Lance gasped and swung the helm hard aport!

On their way to the headland, she filled him in quickly on her detective work so far. Lance responded to the adventure with high spirits.

"Blimey, this could be the most fun I've had since that night we all got carried away at the Hammersmith Palace, and Bobo rammed his foot clear through his bass drum!"

It was a tricky chore getting their scuba gear from the boat into the grotto. Nancy had a brief, uneasy feeling that the hogsheads had been moved slightly from where she and Alan had left them. But she dismissed her suspicions in the excitement of their subterranean adventure.

Lance slithered down the crevice first. After lowering the scuba gear, she joined him.

"What now?" he grinned. "Dive in?"

"Let's check things out a bit first."

Following Nancy's flashlight beam, they made their way along the narrow bank of the underground river. Gradually the walls of the stream bed converged until they could explore no farther on foot.

"Okay, swim we must, I guess," said Nancy.

She had on a bikini under her tank top and jeans. While she was doffing her outer clothing, Lance changed into his wet suit behind her back. Then both strapped on their scuba gear and plunged into the water.

"Fairly warm," Nancy remarked gratefully. "Must be the effect of the Gulf current."

The warmth indicated that the underground stream they were exploring was definitely fed from outside, which in turn confirmed Alan's belief that the level might rise considerably at high tide.

Nancy had brought a small but powerful undersea lantern which served to light their way. After they had swum on the surface a fair distance, the roof of the underground passage began to slope downward until at last there was no air clearance left, and they had to don their scuba masks.

But presently both were able to raise their heads again above water. They removed their mouthpieces so they could talk. "Wonder where we are now." Lance said.

"Quite far under the headland, I should think."

Minutes later, Nancy gasped in surprise. Just ahead, a cylindrical iron cage appeared out of the darkness. "What on earth is that?!"

"I was about to ask you the same thing, luv."

She played her lamp beam over the strange

141

contraption. It seemed to be suspended from the solid rock overhead. Its massive iron bars were rusted and slimed with moss. They could make out what looked like a hinged door.

Lance grasped one of the bars and heaved himself up out of the water. When he tried the latch handle, the door opened easily. Both were amazed.

"Somebody must keep it oiled," said Nancy, reminded of the locked door of the Bluebeard Room.

Lance entered the cage and pulled her up to join him. A short flight of ladderlike metal steps ran upward around the inside of the cage to a small trapdoor in its solid metal roof.

"Any idea where it leads?" Lance asked her.

"I can only guess. One thing's for sure—we must be underneath Penvellyn Castle!"

As they took off their scuba gear to explore further, Nancy shivered with excitement. It was almost uncanny, she thought, how closely events seemed to be bearing out her suspicions!

She felt confident that her "connecting link" theory would also prove correct. A musical trap had been laid for her which almost ended fatally in a quicksand bog—but first she had had to be lured to the engine house by that gleam of light. And what better place to see the gleam than up on the castle tower at night!

Assuming there was, indeed, a connection between the two incidents, the plotters must have *known* she would go up on the tower, and maybe even when, which meant that Lisa had been programmed to decoy her up there!

But if so, Lisa must surely have been acting under hypnotic influence—and only one person, Nancy theorized, was best able to exert such influence.

As these thoughts were passing through her head, Lance was mounting the iron ladder treads. He reached up to push against the small trapdoor. It opened with a creak, and he climbed through the opening. Nancy followed.

They found themselves in a dank stone stairwell.

"Game to go on, luv?"

"Try and stop me!"

The stone steps, grooved by centuries of use, wound endlessly upward. At last they found their way to the top, only to be blocked by a plain wooden panel.

Again Lance pushed, and the panel opened outward. Both caught their breaths at the sight that met their eyes. They were in a beamed and vaulted stone room, richly furnished in antique style.

"If this don't beat all!" Lance tried to sound joking, but his voice was husky with awe.

Nancy swung her lamp around, revealing tapestried walls with gilt sconces, heavy oak and walnut furniture that was medieval in appearance—and before a huge fireplace at one end of the room, what looked like a low stone altar.

On the altar, a ring of candlesticks surrounded a

shiny statuette of gold—a woman glancing at a mirror held in her right hand.

"The mate to the Golden Mab!" murmured Nancy.

She tilted her beam upward, and a huge oil portrait came into view above the mantel. It portrayed a stunningly beautiful girl with long blond tresses and slanty emerald-green eyes, clad in the sumptuous court costume of the early 1700's.

Behind her, in shocking contrast, through dark veils of smoke, loomed a goatish, horned devil!

"Who's that?" Lance queried. "The bird, I mean."

"The one-time witch queen of Polpenny, Lady Phoebe Penvellyn," said Nancy. "She died under torture, and because of her extorted confession, other villagers were burned at the stake."

Lance shuddered. "What jolly tidbits you know!"

"Well, here's another. She's almost an exact double of the present Lady Penvellyn. Phoebe was an American girl, too. She must have been a forebear of Lady Lisa's."

Nancy's gaze turned to a pile of modern-day bales and crates. The bales proved to be marihuana and hashish, while the crates contained plastic bags of cocaine!

Lance gaped. "Where'd this stuff come from?"

"The Polpenny witch coven still exists," said Nancy. "Only now they're more into drugs and drug smuggling than witchcraft. Ian Purcell was recruited into the coven and got hooked. That's how he happened to see the Golden Mab."

"Brilliant sleuthing, my dear!" said a cultivated English voice somewhere behind them.

Nancy turned and gasped. The tapestry on one wall had been pulled aside. Several people were stepping out of an alcove behind it. The speaker was Ivor Roscoe. With him were Ethel Bosinny, Dr. Carradine and, surprisingly, Bobo Evans, as well as two hard-eyed men in stylish suits, each holding a gun.

"Unhappily, Miss Drew," Roscoe went on with a sardonic grin, "your kind of snooping is apt to have fatal results!"

18

Witch Bane

Nancy's initial shock gave way to a rush of fear. Her instincts told her these were ruthless, twisted individuals, but she tried not to panic. "Lance and I seem to have interrupted a business transaction," she said coolly, pointing to the pile of drugs.

"So you have, Miss Drew," said Ethel Bosinny, after lighting a wall sconce, "and we find it most inconvenient. Diane warned Ivor yesterday that something like this might happen."

"And your two friends with guns, I presume, are drug dealers from London. They must have slipped in by posing as sightseers with the tour group, but actually came to pick up more goods. Crooks seldom trust each other, I've noticed, so you each make it a point to come and collect your cut in person."

"What a perceptive little busybody you are!"

"But tell me, Miss Bosinny," Nancy went on, "how did you all get here unnoticed?"

"I was visiting Lisa, my dear. It wasn't hard to slip over to this wing, while pretending to let myself out of the castle. The others came through a secret 'priest-hole' passageway that dates back to the days of Cromwell and King Charles."

"And these drugs you're about to sell were smuggled in by sea the night before last."

Dr. Carradine eyed Nancy suspiciously. "Now how the deuce would you know that?"

"I saw the boatman from my bedroom window," said Nancy. Suddenly she caught her breath. "Oh no! Did you people stop Alan Trevor from showing up at the harbor?"

"Our London friends here attended to him early this morning," said the doctor with a thin smile. "They forced him at gunpoint to swallow a powerful sedative. It knocked him out almost at once. But don't be alarmed, Miss Drew, he'll sleep it off."

"In point of fact," Ethel Bosinny added, "we were hoping his absence might discourage *you*, Nancy dear. But no! You are such a *persistent* little—"

Just then a key grated in the lock. The door opened and Hugh Penvellyn stepped into the Bluebeard Room. He stopped short, gaping in disbelief. "What the devil's going on here?!"

"My!" We seem to be collecting quite a crowd of gate-crashers," said Ivor Roscoe mockingly.

Lord Penvellyn's face darkened with rage. "So you're the filthy witch-cultists who ruined my uncle!"

"These are just the ringleaders," said Nancy. "There are usually thirteen in a coven, so they must have followers in the village, people who are just as much victims as your uncle was, I imagine. *These* witches are more interested in drug smuggling." She gestured to the bales and cartons.

Her words seemed to fill Hugh Penvellyn with fresh fury. He started forward, fists clenched—but the two drug dealers stopped him at gunpoint.

"Don't try anything, Your Lordship," sneered one, "unless you're bored with living in a castle."

"If only you'd stayed away!" purred Ethel Bosinny. "But the damage is done now. I'm afraid we'll have to get rid of you along with these other two bothersome snoops."

"You must be out of your mind!" Hugh retorted contemptuously. "You can't possibly hope to get away with murder—not here in Castle Penvellyn!"

"But of course we can, Hugh dear, if nobody ever finds your bodies. Which they won't, once we've drowned you at high tide in that iron cage down below, like rats in a trap!"

"What are you talking about?!" Hugh growled.

"Nancy will explain while the water's rising."

As the two spoke, Nancy found herself clutching

at a sudden straw of hope. She felt sure she'd heard the faint sound of footsteps ascending the stone stairs. *Could this possibly be the person she prayed it was!?*

If it was, everything depended on warning him in time—and on distracting the crooks' attention.

Quickly she caught Lance's eye and indicated the pile of dope. Then she looked straight at the door through which Hugh had entered, *"Alan!"* she cried. *"Thank goodness you've come!"*

There was instant confusion! Both gunmen turned in the direction Nancy was looking. Lance seized his opportunity. Scooping up a bale, he hurled it with all his might. It struck one of the gunmen on the head, knocking him to the floor!

At that instant, Alan Trevor appeared in the panel opening. He was clad in a diver's wet suit and armed with a boathook.

The other gunman saw him and swung around to fire. But the boathook was already whizzing through the air! It hit the crook in the chest, and he too went down, his gun flying from his hand!

Both Roscoe and Dr. Carradine lunged for the fallen weapons. Hugh kicked one gun out of Ivor's reach and felled him with a vicious right hook. Lance was subduing the doctor.

Ethel Bosinny dashed toward the door, but Nancy snatched up the boathook and tripped her. Ethel went sprawling on the floor, screaming with fury!

149

In moments it was all over. Alan and Lance kept the prisoners covered with the drug dealers' guns while Hugh went to phone the police.

"Oh, Alan, what wonderful timing!" exclaimed Nancy. "But how did you manage to recover from the sedative so soon?"

"The phone rang twice for a very long time," he grinned. "It was ringing practically right in my ear. By the time it stopped, I was out of my fog. When I finally got to Polpenny Harbor, I spied your dinghy over by the headland. Reckon you can work out the rest of it."

"You sure know how to keep a date!" Nancy laughed, and kissed him on the cheek.

"Hey, don't I rate one?" Lance complained, so she kissed him too.

That evening in the castle drawing room, Nancy discussed the case with Lisa and Hugh. Lisa had been deeply shaken when she learned about Ethel Bosinny's role in the witch cult and drug smuggling racket. "How could she have been so nice to me, Nancy—that's what I can't understand!"

"You were important to her, Lisa. The toxin in her herb cordial kept you just unwell enough to need her therapy, and her hypnotic suggestions enabled her to put you in danger at any time, in case Hugh went to the police. She probably hoped to eventually draw you into the coven."

Hugh revealed that his uncle had belonged to the

coven. Shortly before his death, knowing that his nephew would soon inherit both his title and the castle, he had told Hugh everything. But he refused to name the other members of the coven and made Hugh swear to take no action against the cult. Hugh had agreed, provided it ceased to exist.

"But the others obviously never trusted my promise," he went on. "First I received an anonymous phone call, which I now know was made by Roscoe, disguising his voice. He threatened to create a scandal that would ruin my family name if I made any move. Then, after I married Lisa, that drug dealer saw me in London one day and swore his gang would kill her if I talked."

"Had you seen the portrait of Phoebe before you met Lisa?" Nancy asked curiously.

"Yes, and I suppose I fell in love with her before I ever laid eyes on this little witch." Hugh smiled fondly at his wife. "The resemblance was so striking, I knew there must be some family connection."

Nancy related that Ethel had had cult members spread superstitious rumors in the village that Lisa was a reincarnation of the infamous witch queen who had brought such tragedy to Polpenny. "That's why they wouldn't talk to you, Lisa—they were afraid of you."

"Good grief, that's hard to believe in this day and age, Nancy!"

"Not in Cornwall, apparently."

Dr. Carradine had confessed to the police that he was the one who had introduced the coven to drugs. But Nancy believed that Ethel Bosinny was the stronger character, and the one who had built up their profitable drug smuggling racket.

She had drawn the two rock musicians, Ian Purcell and Bobo Evans, into the cult to use them as pushers. Ian had done his best to get off drugs and get out of the cult. When he saw the Golden Mab on a TV documentary show, he realized its mate on the cult's altar was worth a fortune, and tried to cash in on it. Ethel Bosinny ruthlessly had him suspended in the iron cage at high tide, after drugging him, literally frightening him out of his wits.

"What a horrible woman!" Lisa gasped.

"She believed in her own witchcraft, I think," mused Nancy. "She slipped an elf-bolt into a letter you sent your mother, probably after sweetly offering to post it for you, and did the same thing with my letter from Lance Warrick. And after your mother called to say I might be coming over, Ethel had Bobo Evans send me tickets to the Crowned Heads concert and then plant cocaine in my purse."

Lisa shuddered. "It all seems like a bad dream!"

Hugh hugged her. "The nightmare's over now, dear—thanks to Nancy!"

Days later, after a week of sun and fun on the Cornish Riviera, Nancy prepared to fly home. Both Lance and Alan were at Heathrow to see her off. She didn't know that she would soon find herself involved in a frightening mystery called *The Phantom of Venice*.

"You still haven't said which one of us you care for most, Nancy luv!" Lance complained.

A voice announced that it was time to board. Nancy kissed each of her suitors and replied lightly, "I guess that's one riddle I haven't solved yet!"